# 诗一样的安大略
## Ontario in Poems

刘 昭 著译

Written and translated by Dr. Liu Zhao

上海三联书店

Shanghai Joint Cultural Communication Limited

致读者：

欢迎您就本书中的任何疑问联系作者。

To my readers:
    Welcome your contact for any questions in this
book.

我的邮箱：
    E-mail address: drliuzhao@hotmail.com

# 作者简介

刘昭,男,1970年1月生。甘肃天水市人。毕业于南京铁道医学院临床医学系。在大学时发明了微电脑控制的子午流注,灵龟八法和飞腾八法的人体针灸模型,获得国家发明专利。目前获得两项针灸类国家专利,发表医学论文5篇。出版有《汉英对照疑难病中医验案精选》,上海科技出版社;及《汉英对照独穴针灸疗法》,人民卫生出版社。并著有纯英文版《Single-point Acupuncture and Moxibustion Therapy》,人民卫生出版社,发行于欧美多国。2006年以杰出移民身份移居加拿大多伦多并坚持行医至今。

**About author: Dr. Liu Zhao** was born in Tianshui city, Gansu Province, January 1970.He graduated from Nanjing Railway Medical College. As early as his college days, he had gained a national patent for his microcomputer-controlled human body model of Midday-midnight Ebb-flow, the Eightfold Method of Soaring. Currently, he holds two TCM patents and published several academic papers and 3 books: *Chinese-English Elucidation Selected Cases of Obstinate Diseases Treated by Traditional Chinese Medical Therapies* in Shanghai Scientific and Technical Publishers; *Single-point Acupuncture and Moxibustion Therapy* (both Chinese-English and English edited) in People's Medical Publishing House. At present, he resides in Toronto, Canada as a self-employed immigrant and insists on clinic practice.

# 序

　　二零一二年春暖花开之时，收到一个寄自加拿大的邮包，很厚重，邮资不菲。打开来，发现是一部书稿，是向商务印书馆投稿。稿件三百多页，从封面到最后一页，设计精良。正文是中文格律诗、英文诗，配以精美的加拿大安大略山水风景摄影。一口气读了十几页，为作者深厚的中国古典文化底蕴和地道的英文所折服。这才想起要知道作者是何许人，何以能够精通两种语言的文化文学，且能够用最能体现一种语言能量的诗体表现出来？刘昭，一位生活在加拿大的中国中医！

　　可以说，是带着复杂的心情读完这部书稿的。所谓复杂的心情，一是难以置信。难以相信这些诗歌是作者自己用中文古典诗歌格律写就，再用英文写出来。注意，这里我没有使用"翻译"二字。本书中的英文诗不是单纯意义上的翻译诗，它们是作者用同样的内心感受写出来的，亦如作者的中文诗，都是内心情感的抒发。二是自叹不如。本人是英文专业的学生和学者，以英文为学习专业，以英文作为向社会服务的本领。自学会26个字母之日至今，业已近半生时日，无有建树。三是本馆出版方向有限，无法将这部双语原创作品奉献给读者。所以，只得忍痛割爱，荐其在文学出版方面卓有成效的出版社诸如三联出版。刘先生恳请本人为此书作序，几次推脱，不敢担当，且自渐形秽。最后在刘先生的一再请求下，只得勉为其难，答应为这部诗集写上几句话。

　　中国文学，源起诗歌。最简朴直白，也最高深莫测。《红楼梦》里黛玉与香菱的一段对话，可谓将诗歌的精髓暴露无遗。

　　香菱笑道："据我看来，诗的好处，有口里说不出来的意思，想去却是逼真的。有似乎无理的，想去竟是有理有情的。"黛玉笑道："这话有了些意思，但不知你从何处见得？"香菱笑道："我看他《塞上》一首，那一联云：'大漠孤烟直，长河落日圆。'想来烟如何直？日自然是圆的：这'直'字似无理，'圆'字似太俗。合上书一想，倒象是见了这景的。若说再找两个字换这两个，竟再找不出两个字来。"（曹雪芹《红楼梦》第四十八回）

　　涉及山水的古典诗词，有三种意境。一是以山水描写为主，其审美意境蕴含在自然风光之中。"大漠孤烟直，长河落日圆。"（王维《使至塞上》）画面宏阔壮观，缓缓的"升烟"和"落日"产生一种相对的静感，蕴含着生命的永恒。一个"直"，一个"圆"，看似平淡的文字，却溢出深远的意境。"两个黄鹂鸣翠柳，一行白鹭上青天。"（杜甫《绝句》）画面由近至远，色彩搭配更显现出立体的美感，眼前是黄鹂在绿柳中穿梭鸣唱，远处是白鹭在蓝天中列队飞翔。诗中有画，画中有诗，是诗，亦是画。"明月松间照，清泉石上流。"（王维《山居秋暝》）明亮的月光辐射在松林间，明暗分明，清澈的泉水在形态各异的大石小石间穿流，整个景致犹如一幅山水画，清新恬淡。"写景之句，以工致为妙品，真境为神品，淡远为逸品。"（冒春荣《葚原诗说》）王维的此句堪称写景之句中的逸品。

二是以山水为铺垫，与人的经验产生类比，在人的感悟中达到升华。"乱石穿空，惊涛拍岸，卷起千堆雪。"（苏轼《念奴娇·赤壁怀古》）"石"、"涛"、"雪"本是自然界中最为常见的景物；但"穿空"的"乱石"、"拍岸"的"惊涛"、"卷起"的"千堆雪"则使得场面巨动起来，产生一种气势磅礴的效果，将当年群雄鏖战赤壁的场面再现。"大江东去，浪淘尽、千古风流人物。"词人随后借景生情，由景物转为人生，慨叹"江山如画，一时多少豪杰。"这种转变不仅不显得突兀，反而显得是一种必然，是与读者一道产生的共鸣。"东林精舍近，日暮空闻钟。"（孟浩然《晚泊浔阳望庐山》）孟浩然写景，语言简淡疏朗，题材单纯，风格恬淡孤清，情趣高雅脱俗，将主观感受融入自然景观之中，创造出清远拔俗的艺术境界。末尾句是一个时间上的倒叙。字面上看，仿佛是听到东林寺的钟声，方晓得自己已到此地。而那不可言喻的信息是，钟声使诗人的思绪嘎然而止，回到现实之中。东林寺的钟声与诗人的思绪比联，令人产生余音袅袅的效果。"诗至此，色相俱空，真如羚羊挂角，无迹可求，画家所谓逸品是也。"（王士禛《带经堂诗话》）

三是由于人类生活的长期积淀，对自然景物形成了约定俗成的拟人化共同认知。正是这种认知，使得读者对某些山水描写不再形成一幅自然风景画面，而是直接比兴人类的社会生活，几乎对自然景色没有太多的感受，而更多的是自然景物的拟人化产生的效果，完全是写物喻人。"青山依旧在，几度夕阳红。"（杨慎《临江仙》）尽管从文字上看，此句表现的是永恒的自然万物和亘古悠长的宇宙；其实，词人所要表述的绝非自然景观，而是阐释人生哲理。自然与宇宙并不会随着朝代的更迭和人类的生死而改变。相比于自然和宇宙，人世间的是非曲直都是短暂的，古往今来的英雄伟业也不过是人们闲谈的话题。全词在怀古中反思，在景物中言情，阐明哲理、意境深邃，表现出一种大彻大悟的历史观和人生观："古今多少事，都付笑谈中。""花开堪折直须折，莫待无花空折枝。"（杜秋娘《金缕衣》）如果不将人们对自然形成的比联经验加入其中，而是一味考虑字面意义，就无法真正理解此句。诗人告诫人们要珍视时间，及时行乐。人类生存在大自然之中，一山一水，一草一木都与人类的生息相关；而人类文化的起源也是依托着大自然的丰富多彩、千变万化。

"天地与我并生，而万物与我为一。"（《庄子·齐物论》）中华文化强调人与自然的和谐一体，我国最早的诗集《诗经》对大自然山光水色的描写就多采用比兴的手法，借景寓情。"蒹葭苍苍，白露为霜。所谓伊人，在水一方。"（《诗经·秦风》）宜人的景色更突出了女性的美丽动人。纵观中国古典山水诗词，总体来说，诗/词人追求物我两忘的超然境界，"我见青山多妩媚，料青山见我应如是。情与貌，略相似。"（辛弃疾《贺新郎》）这种"情貌相似"绝非单纯的与自然求同，认同"山性即我性"、"水性即我性"，而是要借助人类长期以来对自然界产生的一种从人的角度出发，以人的七情六欲为审视基础而形成的概念，描写自然风景，寄寓人类感怀，抒发审美理念，反映人的思想意识，达到"心移形释，与万物冥合"（柳宗元《永州八记》）的目的。此时的"物我为一"更强调的是"山情即我情"、"水情即我情"，（唐志契《绘事微言·山水性情》）心有所托，意有所归。

"登山则情满于山，观海则意溢于海。"（刘勰《文心雕龙》）诗歌语言的基本特征是意义与意象的融合，是一种更需要创新能力的隐喻语言活动，其核心成分是创新性。情景交融是审美主体感受与自然客体相契合，对客体的自然景观产生心理反应；这样，原本在普通视角下看不出相似的喻体和对象之间随着视角的改变产生链接，形成一种创新的、异于常规的相似性，产生"我见青山多妩媚，料青山见我应如是"的效果，达到形神兼备、借形寓意的艺术境界，正所谓"水声山色，竞来相娱"。（辛弃疾《贺新郎》）乘物以游心，言物以喻情，拓展诗歌的审美空间，营造独特的诗歌意境，达到借客体形象揭示审美主体内在感情的目的。"窗里人将老，门前树已秋。"（韦应物《淮上遇洛阳李主簿》）秋天的树在人的思维影像中是枯萎的黄叶纷纷飘落，曾经枝叶繁茂的绿树在秋风中显得沧桑、颓萎、孤独。以自然规律形成的"树已秋"的影像比联人类的"人将老"，无需再费笔墨，诗中的"窗里人"的形象和心态被展示得一清二楚。李清照的"绿肥红瘦"（《如梦令》）采用借代手法，点出人们通识的"红"指花，"绿"指叶。随后采用比拟手法，借助人们常用的喻指，将"红"和"绿"拟人为女人和男人。"肥"和"瘦"亦如此。枝叶依然茂盛，花儿业已凋零。"绿肥红瘦"便点出了词人的旨意，红颜易逝。

"瞻彼日月，悠悠我思。"（《诗经·邶风》）人类的触景生情，是主体对客体的"感物"、"比兴"，表现了主体心理与客观物象之间的微妙关系。王维是盛唐山水诗的代表人物，他的山水诗静穆淡薄，讲求意境，富有禅趣。他善于发现和捕捉自然景物的形象特征，将自己的主观情感与自然界的客观景物想融合，以绘画技巧构图和着色，托物寓情，象外有象，景外有景，意外有意，韵外有致，有一种悠远的意境。"斜光照墟落，穷巷牛羊归。"（王维《渭川田家》）一幅农家村落的景象跃然纸上。随后出现了"念牧童"的"野老"和"荷锄立"的"田夫"；一个"念"字，一个"立"字，将农村和谐的氛围描绘得淋漓尽致，与朴素静谧的环境浑然一体。此时的诗人犹如正在欣赏这幅山水人物画者，触景生情，"即此羡闲逸，怅然吟式微。"将景致与人的感受巧妙比联，达到以景写人，借景抒怀的境界。"味摩诘之诗，诗中有画；观摩诘之画，画中有诗。"（苏轼《东坡志林》）王维的山水诗写景如画，形神俱佳，气韵生动。"词秀调雅，意新理惬；在泉成珠，着壁成绘，一字一句，皆出常境。"（殷璠《河岳英灵集》）

中国人对"山"和"水"的感受，有着其独特的文化发展背景。孔子曰："夫水者，君子比德焉。""君子见大水必观"是因其似德、似仁、似义、似智、似勇、似察、似包、似善化、似正、似度、似意。（《荀子·宥坐》）庄子描写秋天江河的洪浩意象，"以天下之美尽在己"；（《庄子·秋水篇》）李白的《将进酒》用黄河水奔流直下的气势、以"君不见"的设问形式形象地表达了三层意境：黄河浩荡、生命短暂、人生感悟，"逝者如斯，卒莫消长。"可以说，在中华文化中，水的比兴作用非常宽泛。李白的"抽刀断水水更流"喻指愁绪像水一样无始无终；辛弃疾的"郁孤台下清江水，中间多少离人泪"（《菩萨蛮》）将离乡背井、有家难归的愁苦化作清江水中的离人泪；李煜的"问君能有几多愁，恰似一江春水向东流"（《虞美人》）怀恋故国的山水，表现亡国的愁思；李白的"孤帆远影碧空尽，唯见长江天际流"（《送孟浩然之广陵》）把送别友人、不忍分离的心境通过景观描写而入木三分；白居易的"日出江花红胜火，春来江水绿如蓝"（《望江南》）把对江南美景的回味与思乡之情联系在一起，"怎不忆江南？"在李白的笔下，"桃花潭水深千尺，不及汪伦送我情"，（《赠汪伦》）深厚的友情比千尺的潭水还深；秦观的《鹊桥仙》把情人之爱比作"柔情似水"。

"仓颉之初作书，盖依类象形。"（许慎《说文解字·叙》）汉字属于表意的词素音节文字，汉字的象形使汉字本身具有形象感，有明显的直观性和表意性。因此，中国古典诗歌的语言讲求精炼，尽量以最少的字词表现最多的内容。马致远的《天净沙》便是最佳例证。由于汉语的意合性使汉语语言在形态上相对自由，语序灵活，词语组合多变，因此以汉语文字为载体的中国诗歌易于写意。相比而言，英语语言有繁复的时态、语态等，重视句子成分之间的关系，在表达上相对比较严谨，不如汉语灵活。两种语言的差异导致了文学翻译，特别是诗歌翻译难以保持原有诗体风格，难以确切达意。美国诗人罗伯特·弗罗斯特认为，"诗者，译之所失也。"中国古典诗歌凝练的语言，厚重的意象，导致其在转变为另一种语言时，必定会丢失一些精华。因此，对诗歌翻译始终无法达到像其他文体作品那样，在另一种语言中很好地展现出原语的风格、内容等。另一方面，文化差异阻隔了一种语言下的意象正确地输入至另一种语言中。同为月亮，在拟人中却发生了很大的变化。中国文化中拟人的月亮是冰肌玉容的美女，而在德语文化中月亮常常是沉着稳健的男人。

中国有记载的最早诗歌翻译应该是约公元前 540 年的《越人歌》（刘向《说苑·善说》），是将壮文译为汉文。将中国古典作品翻译成英文，最早最具权威的译者当数英国汉学家詹姆斯·理雅各。早在 19 世纪中叶，他便开始翻译中国古典名著，他的《中国经典》包括《大学》、《中庸》、《论语》、《孟子》、《诗经》、《书经》、《礼记》、《易经》、《春秋》、《左传》等。为了能够使其译作达意，理雅各在行文中添加大量的注解，并注重对多义词根据内容采取不同的翻译。如《论语》中的"君子"一词就有十几种表达方式。

翻译是一种语言转换活动，语言是文学的载体，语言结构制约人的思维结构，形成不同的文化样式。将一种语言的文学作品译介为另一种语言的文学作品时，要考虑语言的差异，还要考虑文化的差异，力求最大限度地保存原文所蕴涵的异域文化特色。中国古典英译中，无对等词是一种常见情况。译者在翻译时多采用近义词语加注解、近义词名词化、音译加注解、造词、音译等。以"道"字为例，由于英语中无对等词，以前多译成 way，course，practice，characteristics，truth，doctrine 等，现在多采用音译。有些比喻性意象，考虑到东西方的审美差异，译时要变通，改成符合译入语文化和审美情趣的意象。例如，"山河破碎风飘絮，身世浮沉雨打萍。"（文天祥《过零丁洋》）此句中的"山河"指的是"国家"，可考虑翻译为 mother-land，land 等。如果在译入语中将"山河"译作mountain and river，将会使母语为译入语的读者不知所云。

中国古代汉语中有大量多义的单音词，其语法功能较为灵活，句法中也多有省略。因此，中国格律诗讲求语言精炼，常省略人称及主语，产生一种客观的、普遍意义的抒情效果，使个人体验上升为普遍的或象征的意蕴，从而使读者也能置身其中，产生更大范围的共鸣。王维《鹿柴》中的"空山不见人，但闻人语声"既可以是某个个体的感受，同时也是人类作为整体所共有的感受。李白《静夜思》中通篇未见个体的表征，但却能使每个人都有同感，一种人类集体的共性。这种现象甚至在表现最具个性的爱情诗中依然如故。《诗经》中有"一日不见，如三秋兮"（《诗经·采葛》）的千古绝唱，虽未点出个体，却是每个人的感受。与汉语不同，英语语言注重语法结构，诗歌中使用人称代词的频率远高于中文诗歌。苏格兰高地诗人罗伯特·彭斯的《我的爱人是一朵红红的玫瑰》，第一行便出现了人称代词"我"。因此，译者不仅要具备一定的译入语水平，同时还要了解以译入语为载体的文化。"译者将全文神理，融会于心，则下笔抒词，自善互备。"（严复《天演论》）

英国桂冠诗人约翰·德莱顿提出诗歌翻译的"三分法"。他认为，一个优秀的诗歌翻译家，首先必须是一位优秀的诗人。本书作者刘先生的双语诗集，其双语不是通常人们所说的"汉译英"，或者"英译汉"，其中的诗歌是诗人用两种语言对同一主题的原创。因此，无论是用中文写出来的诗歌，还是用英文写出来的诗歌，都不存在由于两种语言翻译，特别是对两种语言的诗体文本的翻译而出现的问题。同样是描述同一景观中清澈的湖水，英文不必将就汉语象形表意的文字特点和词句练达的行文风格，而任由英文的语法严谨和行文随意简单的特色；同样是抒发对城堡历史的怀旧情愫，诗人在为中文诗字斟句酌时，无需考虑与英文诗的对等表述，只要诗篇能够意达以寓意深刻、情至以抒发胸怀，便是完美。

二十世纪初是西学东渐之时，中国的志士仁人怀着一腔热血，抱着兴我中华的理想，将西方先进的文化文学、先进的科学技术引介给我民。二十一世纪，世人正在见证东学西渐。越来越多的人学习汉语，对中华五千年璀璨的文化文学情有独钟。在这样的大环境下，笔者希望有更多的人，能像刘先生一样，以两种语言原创诗歌的形式，描画美好的风光，弘扬世界文化。

是为序。

栾奇
二零一三年三月八日
于丹青府

# 前　言

在我幼年学语的时候，父母亲就教我念诵"床前明月光，疑似地上霜"；"鹅，鹅，鹅，曲项向天歌"等等诗歌。那时候能在亲友的面前背诵出几首诗歌，是一件多么令人自豪的事啊。多年以后，每当朋友的孩子在我面前背诵出一首首唐诗宋词的时候，我会情不自禁的去拥抱这些可爱的小朋友，因为这让我在心底荡漾着一份幸福和温暖。

诗歌对于我们这个民族，国家，犹如甘甜的母乳，滋养着我们内心深处最柔软，最纯净的那块地方。从幼年的呱呱习语，到少年时的努力进取，青年时的成家立业，直至成年后的艰辛劳作和老年后的安享晚年，诗歌犹如灵魂，贯穿着我们整个的生命！曾记否？"锄禾日当午，汗滴禾下土"，"少壮不努力，老大徒伤悲"的教诲？"慈母手中线，游子身上衣"的牵挂？"青青子衿，悠悠我心"的相思？更有"行到水穷处，坐看云起时"的人生独行，以及"会当凌绝顶，一览众山小"的人生豪迈。瑰丽奇妙的祖国诗歌，在我们人生中的每一个阶段都留下了深刻的烙印。这就是祖国传统诗歌文化的生命力和魅力！她就像母亲甘甜的乳汁，滋养着我们一代代人的成长。

古老的传统诗歌是如此的优美，如何让传统诗歌这枝奇葩在新的时代中绽放出新的活力，并让世界上更多的人们所接受，这是每一位热爱祖国传统文化的学者所共同面临的一个问题。本书即是作者对这一问题所做的一个尝试性的解答。

《诗一样的安大略》一书是作者在长期学习和吸收了前辈诗家宝贵的创作经验的基础上，用中国传统诗歌的创作手法对加拿大安大略省的山水风光进行的一个系统性的文学描述。所描述的对象，包括了安大略省所有著名的国家公园，省级公园和自然保护区，以及多伦多市市内及周边地区极富特色的一些社区公园。在本书中，这些内容用中英两种文字，配合作者实地拍摄的照片，进行了三位一体的具体展现。这在祖国诗歌发展的历史上，尚属首次。这也清晰的表明：在时隔千百年之后，在远离本土的异国他乡，中华传统诗歌仍然具有着勃勃的生命力，仍然在照亮着远方游子的心。

本书的内容主要分为三个部分：中文原创诗歌，英文翻译，及其所属的相关配图。

在本书的中文原创诗歌部分，作者严格遵循古体诗歌的创作审美标准，将唐宋诗家高超的诗词写作技法认真学习，在融会贯通的基础上运用到自己山水诗歌的创作中来。在形式上，以古律，古绝为主，借鉴格律诗的一些特点，从而在声韵上整体做到仄起平入，通顺上口；同时不以一字一句而拘泥，避免了以律害意，自缚手脚。这样做，一方面在诗歌创作上严格继承了唐宋诗家的思想灵魂，另一方面也避免了固步自封式的"诗八股"。这种创作理念，贯穿于本书写作的始终。作者认为，在继承发扬祖国传统文化的时候，我们不应该拘泥于形式而忽视了内涵，真正的继承不但在于得其形，更重要的是得其神。

本书的第二部分是英文翻译。目前在国内外，古体诗的翻译著作并不很多，这也给作者学习如何正确翻译古体诗的过程带来了一定难度。尽管如此，作者也尽可能的收集一些已出版的相关作品认真学习，这中间主要学习的对像是英译本的"唐诗三百首"，"宋词三百首"等，也包括一些纯英文的古体诗歌，如莎士比亚的"十四行"等。通过这些学习，本人基本上掌握了英文诗的写作特点和规律，并将这些学习所得运用到自己的英译过程中。尽量做到译文准确，声韵通顺。当然，作为一个既非英语母语，又非英语专业的职业医生，要从事这件工作的难度是可想而知的，所以这中间发生的纰漏也是不可避免的。这里作者真诚的告诉大家：本书的出版，仅仅是起一个开端的作用。作者希望通过本书的出版，能够起到抛砖引玉的作用，以吸引更加优秀的人才来继承和发展祖国的传统诗歌文化。敬请大家对此谅解。

本书的第三部分内容是每首诗歌所配的图片。这些图片全部是作者实地所拍摄的第一手材料。这些照片来源真实，它们真实的再现了每一首诗的具体创作环境，它们是对一首首诗歌最客观的实际注解。这些照片，尽管不能和职业摄影师的摄影艺术作品相媲美，但他们绝对真实。是作者实际观察到的原生态的景色。这些图片，有些是作者长途跋涉而得来，有的是在一瞬间由手机抢拍而来。作者将这些原生态的图片配在每一首诗的下面，是想用事实告诉读者：诗意的人生就在我们身边，不用刻意追求寻找。

本书写作过程历时近 3 年，中间受到多位朋友的帮助，尤其多伦多张志华先生和上海的施炳煌先生为本书的出版提供了巨大帮助，在此表示由衷的谢意！

愿祖国传统诗歌源远流长于世！

愿天下人共享诗意人生！

刘 昭

2012 年 8 月 10 日于加拿大多伦多

# Foreword

In my early childhood, when I began babbling, my parents taught me a few ancient poems such as "So bright the moonlight sheds to my bed, just like the frost on the ground" and "Swan, swan, swan, stretching their necks and singing to the sky". At that time, I was so proud of myself when I recited these poems to my parents' friends. Today, when my friends' kids recite these poems to me, I can't help giving them a hug, for the incredible happiness and warmness rippling in my heart.

To us, the folks who are raised up in China, poem is like mother's milk nourishing the softest and purest place in our heart. While we grow from a babbling toddler to a rebellious teenager, from an established adult to a relaxed senior, traditional chinese poems(TCP) have become part of our soul, accompanying our life all the way through.

As you might remember, we learned life instructions from "Hoeing the grass under the noonday sun, His sweat drips on the ground" and "Invest no effect when young and strong, harvest nothing but regret and pang", love from "The thread in a caring mother's hands, becomes the sweater of the travelling son" and "Cyan is the edge of thy coat, rippling was deep in my heart", and state of mind from "Travel to where the river ends, sit up and watch the cloud rises" and "Once the mountain top is conquered, all peaks are belittled".

Such beautiful poems have been not only inspiring and guiding us at every step of our life, but nurturing our soul generation after generation. No doubt, it's the best manifestation of the charm and strong vitality of TCP.

In this new era, while pace of life is speeding up and new forms of art are emerging every day, the challenge to every scholar who loves traditional Chinese culture is how to rejuvenate TCP so more people in the world would accept them and appreciate them. In fact, this book is an attempted solution to meet the challenge.

*Ontario in poems*, bilingual in Chinese and English, vividly depicted the famous scenery spots in Ontario, Canada in the style of TCP. Blending the valuable composing experiences of senior poets and my own, I was able to magnify the natural beauty of the famous national parks, provincial parks, and conservation areas in Ontario. (Note: some characteristic parks in Toronto and adjacent areas are also included).

In this book, every piece of scenery is presented to readers in both Chinese and English with the photographs taken by myself – a unique three-in-one composing style that has never been applied in the history of TCP. Such a practice is a clear proof that, regardless the history of thousands of years, the spirit of TCP is still vibrant and strong, lightening the hearts of the travelers abroad who are thousands of miles away from the origin of the spirit.

This book is composed of three parts: original Chinese poems, translated English version, and the related photographs.

In the first part, my composition strictly follows the aesthetic standard of TCP. Based on in-depth study and thorough comprehension of the senior poets' composing skills, I've developed my own style, which was then skillfully applied to my scenery poems.

Tones and rhymes are essential in TCP. The ancient tone-freed rhymes, including the rhyme of four sentences and eight sentences, are often seen in the book. However, some ancient tone-restricted rhymes are also absorbed into my composing practice. For instance, the rhyme of a sentence begins from descent tone and ends in ascent one, creating a smooth but wavelike reciting experience.

Such a composing style not only carries on the soul of TCP but also prevent authors from paying excessive attention to build a rhyme in a stereotyped word-by-word fashion. Carrying the composing principle throughout my poem writing process, I firmly believe that, in the process of studying and inheriting the art of TCP, the most important thing is not imitating its style, but grasping its spirit.

The second part is the translated English version. Translating TCP from Chinese to English has been a well-known tough job thanks to the language and culture difference. Even the published monographs about this topic can hardly be found in the library or bookstores. Nevertheless, I managed to learn the essence of English poem writing from a few classic books, including Chinese-English bilingual version of 300 Tang Poems and 300 Song Poems, as well as the original Sonnets written by W.William Shakespeare.

Not a native English speaker or an English majored scholar, I was able to deliver the translation in an accurate and smooth manner with these efforts, although it's far from perfect. I would encourage my readers to correct any possible errors in this book. But more importantly, I would like to voice my vision to every reader of this book: "Publishing this book is merely a beginning of my cast-away-a-brick-to-attract-a-jadestone journey. I hope my works would inspire the gifted talents to join the club of studying and inheriting TCP so there will be more excellent works in the future."

The third part of this book is the photographs related to the poems. 100% taken by myself, the photos revealed the vivid environment in which the poems were composed. Literally, they are the actual annotations for every poem. Not to match any professional art works, the photographs, some of which were taken with cell phone in difficult situations, genuinely share with you my views and feelings at the very moment. I have illustrated the poems with these live photos to deliver an important message: Poetic living needs no painstaking seeking because it is just around us.

It took me over three years completing this book. In the process, many warm-hearted friends offered me great supports , especially Mr. Zhang, Zhihua in Toronto and Mr. Shi, Binghuang in Shanghai strongly supports me. I'm sincerely grateful to all of them.

May TCP blossom and grow in the new busy world.

May everyone under the sun enjoy a life in poems.

Dr. Liu Zhao
August,2012 in Toronto, Canada

# 目录 contents

# 圣劳伦斯群岛国家公园

圣劳伦斯群岛国家公园里岩石堆积的岛屿，海风吹拂的松树林，以及阴凉的水域使其有着北部粗旷的风味，它位于多伦多东部，距多伦多仅仅几个小时的车程。这里是原著人 Mississauga Anishinaabe 和 Haudenosaunee 传统的夏季家园，自然和文化交融的地方。雄伟的城堡和历史悠久的避暑山庄与高低不平的花岗岩岛屿还有松树林交相辉映。

# St. Lawrence Islands National Park

The rocky islands, windswept pines, and cool waters of St. Lawrence Islands National Park have the flavour of the northern wilderness just a few hours east of Toronto. In this traditional summer home of Haudenosaunee and Mississauga Anishinaabe, nature and culture intermingle. Majestic castles and historic summer homes stand in contrast to rugged islands of granite and pine.

011

# 千岛湖

菩萨脱下翡翠裙，化出碧波绿水晶。

水清尚嫌无好景，璎珞随手撒其中。

风吹万点琉璃绿，夕照一湖玛瑙红。

轻舟一叶来览胜，秀色满湖湿翠衿。

# Thousand Islands Lake

Long long ago, a Bodhisattva spreaded out her jade-coloured skirt,

varied it into a whole lake of green crystal water.

But all of this wasn't her expectant work of art,

then she cast jade necklace into the lake apart.

As breeze blowing, thousand islands seem as floating green lazurite.

In sunset shining, a whole lake looks like rippling red agate.

Such scenery attracted me coming by a brisking boat.

The elegant scenery wet my blue coat and influenced my heart.

# 千岛湖大桥

琴弓绕塔穿云过，垂下弦丝百千条。

碧波摇曳水云路，秋风拂动箜篌桥。

水流东西浮千岛，桥贯南北通两国。

枫叶如火秋正好，水色山光映素袍。

# Thousand Islands Bridge

Bow tied to the towers, a transverse harp is hanging in cloud.

From which, hundreds bowstrings vertically hang down in wind.

Clear river ripples the graceful shadow of the bridge overhead.

When breeze blowing, it seems as performing the natural sound.

River flows from west to east, it floats thousand islands inside.

Bridge crosses from north to south, two countries are connected.

In so beautiful autumn, the aflame maples redden all hills around.

My white robe is floating around while my heart is so influenced.

# 千岛湖瞭望塔

塔高白云落，风劲海川摇。

天阔衔远树，水渺入海潮。

烟波藏千岛，云径化一桥。

秋风声瑟瑟，红叶正萧萧。

# Thousand Islands Skydeck

The tower is so high that the white clouds fly under the deck.

Winds are so broad that the whole valley is almost in rock.

Vast sky covers all the trees along the river bank.

River flows far away till converging into Atlantic.

Thousand charming islands are hidden in flying mist and smoke.

A long road in cloud varies into a big bridge across the lake.

Wind blowing through, islands in river rustle and chink.

While aflame maple leaves redden all over the hill peak.

# 钻微颗小岛

碧水何悠悠，浮动两小洲。

桥长四五步，水环三两周。

湖如碧玉镜，岛似绿簪头。

神仙居于此，湖天逍遥游。

# Zavikon Island

What a leisurely blue lake!

Two little islands rippling in it.

The tiny bridge is only four or five feet.

Clean water surrounding just as rippling silk.

Blue smooth lake is jade mirror alike.

Islands are like green hearpins' tip in link.

The immortal living here owns so much luck.

Day by day, he freely travels from sky to lake.

# 心岛城堡

伊人若秋水，水流人已非。

秋波盈盈去，红叶点点飞。

岛拳如心迹，楼空似人悲。

系舟青枫岸，待人乘月归。

# Boldt Castle on Heart Island

The lady of past was clean as water of fall.

Water is still flowing while she is in dream all.

Flowing of river is rippling away along the shore.

Red leaves are flying in air more and more.

Outline of the island is just as a heart in woe.

His deep sorrow suffuses the empty hall.

Oh, dear guy, please tie a canoe to the maple shore,

by which your honey would come back under moonlight bow.

# 秋游千岛湖

一袭水色宝蓝裙，上簪万点碧玲珑。

清风吹起千褶翠，白云拂动一湖青。

故垒依稀人不在，楼台参差岛半空。

天上人家居于此，水月光中梦良辰。

# Travelling Thousand Islands Lake in Autumn

What a watery sapphire skirt!

On which thousand exquisite jades are inlaid apart

When breeze blows, thousands layers of ripples are so verdant.

In clean lake, the reflections of innumerous clouds are so white.

The dreamlike lady passed away but her castle is still as the past.

Buildings and platforms stand ruggedly and most islands are desolate.

The nobles select so elegant place as their cosy nest.

Sleeping in watery moonlight here, even the dreams are all excellent.

# 布鲁斯半岛国家公园

　　布鲁斯半岛国家公园坐落于布鲁斯半岛北端，在格鲁吉亚湾和休伦湖之间。这个美丽的公园，拥有 155 平方公里的面积，位于尼亚加拉大断壁的顶尖角，由石灰岩峭壁、洞穴和地下溪流，以及加拿大最古老的一些树木的原始森林组成。布鲁斯半岛国家公园是由一系列令人难以置信的动植物栖息环境组成，从罕见的 alvar 地质带到茂密的森林和清澈的湖泊。这些形成了一个很大的生态系统，是安大略省南部所剩最大的一块自然栖息地。

# Bruce Peninsula National Park

The Bruce Peninsula National Park is situated on the northern tip of the Bruce Peninsula, between Georgian Bay and Lake Huron. The beautiful park, with a size of 155 square kilometers at the tip of the Niagara Escarpment, consists out of limestone cliffs, caves and underground streams, and ancient forests with some of the oldest trees in Canada. The Bruce Peninsula National Park is comprised of an incredible array of habitats from rare alvars to dense forests and clean lakes. Together these form a greater ecosystem - the largest remaining chunk of natural habitat in southern Ontario.

# 过休伦湖

半天风雨满湖烟，轻舟一叶上蓬山。

灵石曳曳擎霄汉，灯塔萤萤隔水天。

湖心一攒纯碧翠，浪头千卷尽苍蓝。

一身尘劳都洗尽，万里湖天心湛然。

# Sailing on Lake Huron

Drizzling for half a day, all the lake suffuses the fog and mist.

It's so soothing for us to go the fairyland by a brisk boat.

What a miraculous stone! It towers into the sky so tall and straight.

Shining brightly, the lighthouse separates water from the sky at night.

Essence of whole lake gestates the green mid island, it is just so cute.

Waves roll and spread layer by layer, they are so purely blue in my sight.

Toils in my life are entirely washed away in so elegant environment.

The vast clean sky and crystal water refresh my weary heart.

# 花瓶岛

大士何故太匆然？留下净瓶水涯边。

瓶中泻出琉璃水，水里化成翡翠山。

波澜荡漾咏梵呗，云光曼妙示佛天。

慈尊神迹今何在？湖天悠悠水云间。

# Flower Pot Island

Avalokitesvara, you left here so hastily, what is it for?

So that you left your pure bottle on the shore!

from which the lazurite-coloured water is just being in pour,

in which a jade-like island was varied out so verdantly tall.

Like being chanting, wide winds blow clean ripples wow by wow.

As if hinting mystic meaning, clouds leisurely drift row by row.

However, where can we currently find the Bodhisattva at all?

Oh, from lake to sky, she would be concerned with you when you call.

029

# 霹雳角国家公园

　　位于安大略省温莎市东南部 50 公里（30 英里）的加拿大霹雳角国家公园，是加拿大最小的国家公园之一。但这个小小的绿洲每年吸引约 300 万名游客。一个薄薄的三角形伸进伊利湖中，成为加拿大的最南端。

# Pelee Point National Park

Located 50 km (30 miles) south-east of Windsor, Ontario, Point Pelee National Park of Canada is one of Canada's smallest national parks, and yet this tiny green oasis attracts approximately 300 000 visitors each year. A thin triangle jutting into Lake Erie is the southernmost point of Canada.

# 霹雳角

长岬如戟劈海流，天涯到此即尽头。

水分东西显动静，国开南北任往留。

海云寂寂侵远树，客心渺渺近中秋。

日落天涯何处是？月映秋波似客愁。

# Pelee Point

The long cape is so sharp just as a halberd splitting the vast water.

Year by year traveling in the remote corner, but here is just the limit.

From east to west, the sea is divided into half surging and half silent.

Two countries adjoin in south and north, people stay or go as they select.

Trees are standing along the bank, in the vast sky clouds drift and drift.

Moon Festival approaching, my heart with homesickness just beat and beat.

In this remote cape, who could know where the sun is sinking in the west?

I only see the moon shadow shivering in water, just as my lonely heart.

033

# 荷荡

云水一天齐，秋潭双鹭飞。

轻舟三叶去，芦荷四面围。

荷花清若水，芦叶细如眉。

行舟入荷荡，沾得荷露归。

# Lotus Lake

Cloud and water melt into sky as a whole.

Herons flying high there are two.

In the small lake three canoes freely flow.

From four sides lotus and reeds ruffle in row.

Clean like water, lotus is quietly pure.

Thin as eye-brow, reed leaves are soft and low.

Among the lotus my canoe moves so slow.

Because the lotus dews wet my shirt when I go.

# 秋湖观鸟

潭小芦荷盛，天高行雁鸣。

水清鸭弄影，气暖燕栖身。

苍鹭栖芦荡，孵卵卧草深。

舟来忽惊起，乘风过湖东。

# View Birds in Autumn Lake

In small lake, lush reed and lotus are to be bloom.

In high sky, rows of geese cry aloud when they move.

In clean water, ducks are swimming with no fear and shame.

Swallows still stay here for air is so warm.

Resting in deep reeds, two herons are so calm.

They are quietly brooding in their cave.

Suddenly they are frightened when the canoes come.

By a wind, they fly up to the east of lake across a stream.

# 塘莲

日出塘莲静，

秋水玉玲珑。

迎风绽黄蕊，

凌波动素鬟。

# Lotus in Pond

Lotus flowers are quietly blooming in sunrise shining.

Its graceful shadows in cool water is so clean.

As wind blowing, the yellow pistils are entirely open.

The beautiful flowers slightly sway with river rippling.

# 尼亚加拉大瀑布风景区

尼亚加拉大瀑布是三个横跨加拿大安大略省和美国纽约州之间的国际边界瀑布的总称，这一瀑布群也形成了尼亚加拉峡谷的南端。从最大到最小，三个瀑布依次是，马蹄瀑布，美国瀑布和新娘婚纱瀑布。瀑布群位于伊利湖水流入安大略湖的尼亚加拉河上，形成了世界上流量最高的瀑布，具有超过165英尺的垂直落差。马蹄瀑布是北美最有威力的瀑布（按落差高度和流量比）。瀑布群位于多伦多东南偏南75英里。

# Niagara Falls Park

Niagara Falls is the collective name for three waterfalls that straddle the international border between the Ontario and the New York, also forming the southern end of the Niagara Gorge. From largest to smallest, the three waterfalls are the Horseshoe Falls, the American Falls and the Bridal Veil Falls. Located on the Niagara River which drains Lake Erie into Lake Ontario, the combined falls form the highest flow rate of any waterfall in the world, with a vertical drop of more than 165 feet. Horseshoe Falls is the most powerful waterfall in North America. The falls are located 75 miles south-southeast to Toronto.

# 尼亚加拉大瀑布

万方宾客来此行，一览瀑布竟何容？

千匹白练银似泻，万钧雷霆雪样崩。

百丈悬梯攀崖走，一轮渡舟穿浪行。

流云随水渐归去，彩虹如梦横碧空。

# Niagara Falls

Visitors from all come here to see the famous fall.

They eagerly want to know how about it at all.

Hundreds miles of silvery silk are being in pour.

Facing snow slide, thousands decibels rumbling aloud roll.

On steep cliff, bending stairs extend from the low to the tall.

On surging river, a boat is floating for the exciting tour.

Flying cloud and flowing water melt into a charming scroll.

Across the blue sky, there is a dreamful rainbow.

# 夜观尼亚加拉大瀑布

天上今夜挂宝帘，碧霄垂下五彩绢。

虹光浮动起幽梦，霓裳荡漾出斑斓。

水声华彩响仙乐，霞光云影动波澜。

恍然忘却身是客，氤氲缭裳满襟衫。

# Enjoying Niagara Falls at Night

Jewelry curtain in Heaven is hanging tonight.

In clear sky, the falling iridescent silk is so brilliant

Rainbow shining as mystic dream is floating in my sight.

Rosy clouds just like gorgeous ripples charm my heart.

Rumbling sounds of falls are incomparably magnificent.

With rippling, lustrous shadows of cloud gracefully undulate.

Lured by the scenery so much that I forget I'm a guest,

although mists and frost diffusing in air wet my blue coat.

# 瀑布日出

天河老龙吐红珠，

莹莹一颗水中出。

凌波冉冉入云际，

霞光如火冰河苏。

# Sunrise of Niagara Falls

Old dragon is gushing its bloody pearl out of water.

It is so brilliant and glittering at dawning hour.

Rising slowly in sky, it lightens the cloudy weather.

Its aflame luster awakens the frozen heavenly river.

047

# 冰酒

霜华渗入紫水晶，

酿出莹莹冰雪纯。

浓香一滴沁心脾，

凉胸澈腹透冰清。

# Icewine

Essence of frost seeps into purple crystal grapes in growing.

Finally they are brewed into glittering icewine.

Even a drop is so fragrant that it refreshes my heart and spleen.

Cooling me from chest to belly, it is just snowy clean.

# 韦伯斯特瀑布保护区

　　韦伯斯特瀑布保护区位于尼亚加拉大断壁上的安大略省登打士市，是安大略省汉密尔顿地区的一个组成部分。这一保护区以它提供了很具观赏价值的汉密尔顿风景，还有两个很容易从林间小路接近的瀑布而著名。

# Webster's Falls Conservation Area

Webster's Falls Conservation Area is located on the Niagara Escarpment in Dundas, Ontario, a constituent community of Hamilton, Ontario. It is renowned for offering spectacular views of Hamilton and for containing two major waterfalls that are easily accessible via a system of trails.

# 吐丝瀑布

谁家垂秋帘，玲珑响碧天。

素珠千滴下，银丝百尺悬。

清涟穿崖树，氤氲起凉潭。

凭栏遥相看，山青水澹然。

# Tew's Fall

In later autumn whose curtain hangs so high?

The sound is so clear in blue sky.

Thousand pearls drop down in a long line.

Hundreds feet of pure silk looks as a silvery tie.

Through trees on cliff, clean water quickly passes by.

From cool pond, diffusing mists slowly fly.

By rail, I deeply enjoy the view and forget to retire.

Because blue hill and clean water seize my eye.

# 韦伯斯特瀑布

碧潭临深渊，轰然落秋山。

千钧喷雪浪，百丈泻银泉。

瀑流双折素，涧溪三秋寒。

红叶满山落，林阴水自喧。

# Webster's Fall

Top of the deep valley is a smooth blue pond.

Water in it rushes down with great rumble sound.

Snowy waves erupt with thousand decibels rumbling aloud.

Silvery spring pour down from hundred feet of cliff around.

Pure silk turns into two sections shining in the bend.

In later autumn, stream in valley becomes just cold.

Red maple leaves begin to fall down all over the land.

When sunset coming, stream still sings in forest shade.

# 阿岗昆省级公园

阿岗昆省级公园在安省中部，夹在乔治亚湾和渥太华河之间，于 1893 年设立，是加拿大第一个省级公园。园区总面积达 7653 平方公里。是很多人夏季野营的首选地，但每年的名额有限，必须在网上提前预约。

# Algonquin Provincial Park

Algonquin Provincial Park is a provincial park located between Georgian Bay and the Ottawa River. Established in 1893, it is the oldest provincial park in Canada. Additions, since its creation have increased the park to its current size of about 7653 square kilometers. In summer, it's most favorite camping site, but it's so rare that people can only get it by internet ordering in advance.

# 阿岗昆

瑶台宝镜落尘寰，碎作万点碧瀛然。

秋水莹莹千潭月，浮云霭霭一长天。

野树参差藏幽径，澄波潋滟荡秋船。

山苍水绿人无倦，醉卧松荫任流连。

# Algonquin

Jewelry mirror in Heaven fell down on the Earth,

broke into thousand verdant glittering pieces .

Moon in sky varies thousand reflections shining in all lakes,

while rows of  clouds are drifting in boundless space.

Wild trees grow lushly but narrow paths hide insides.

Canoes float on lakes as crystal water gently ripples.

Guests from all enjoy the clean water and blue mountains,

Under the pines, they entirely revel in so graceful views.

# 白鱼湖

白鱼湖水蓝，凝作碧玉簪。

簪上流翡翠，染绿一湖天。

行舟入天镜，推波动画帘。

横棹随水荡，盈手掬鱼莲。

# Whitefish Lake

What a whitefish lake, it ripples so blue water,

its essence gestates a small jade-like island  in shiver,

from which verdancy flows into lake and river,

sky and water are dyed verdant in cloudy weather.

My canoe seems to be flowing on heavenly mirror.

Paddling slowly, we shake the charming painted paper.

Lying paddle on the bow, let canoe ripple as ripples waver.

Then my hands could freely hold fish and lotus flower.

# 波多湖

山小如枕台，水柔可盈怀。

千松一色秀，青峦两边排。

日落莲花静，月隐星河开。

塘蛙声几许？传入帐中来。

# Pog Lake

Small hills are so cute just as my pillow.

Crystal water is so pure it cleans my soul.

Thousands pines sway there in one style show.

Blue hills stand quietly in both sides row.

In sunset shining, blooming lotuse are quietly pure.

Moon hides away while bright stars still glow.

How long have frogs been singing as rivers flow?

It gets into my dream whatever it's high or low.

# 野宿

傍松支罗帐，依水系舟樯。

烹肴充远饥，点火驱晚凉。

水面七份饱，清茶三盏香。

松荫深寂寂，旅人入梦乡。

# Camping

Under the pines, we set up the tent.

By the river, we tie the boat.

Being hungry in the field, we cook greens and meat.

Campfire is lighted up to expel cold in night.

Feeling perfect, noodles satisfy seven tenth of appetite.

Drinking tea brewed three times, we just enjoy the best.

Pine shadows are so deep and silent,

in which we are staying with a satisfied rest.

# 河荡

水滑若凝脂，草柔如青丝。

挥棹起碧浪，穿塘入小池。

水鸟啼远近，野树横高低。

翠羽新孵卵，往来有几时？

# Small River

Smooth water as bitty cream is so rare.

Water grasses are floating like soft hair.

On clear ripples, who being paddling is a free fare.

From lake to pond, canoe is flowing with no care.

Singing ahead or behind,  birds are flying everywhere.

Growing crosswise or vertically, trees diffuse fresh air.

The green bird is brooding with no fear.

No matter I go or come, it always stay there.

# 石湖

嶙石立青溪，绿水绕闸堤。

穿闸两岸阔，入云一天低。

鸟飞水天外，人坐枫下栖。

倚石观云落，隔水望岛矶。

# Stony Lake

Huge stones apart stand in the river.

The sluice is surrounded by clear water.

Passing the sluice, its channel expands wider.

Flowing into clouds, river and sky become lower.

Flying out of my view, the bird is a free flyer.

Resting in shadow of maple, I'm a tired traveler

Leaning on a stone and watching cloud drifting over,

In the rapid river, those huge stones stably tower.

# 基尔贝尔省级公园

　　基尔贝尔省级公园（又称"杀熊省级公园"）位于安大略省的乔治亚湾的东岸，最近的城镇为 Nobel。公园里的那些崎岖山区，岩石滩和松树林景色诱人，适合徒步远足，单车，钓鱼和野营，深受南部的安大略居民喜爱。

# Killbear Provincial Park

Killbear Provincial Park is a park located on Georgian Bay in Parry Sound District, Ontario, near the town of Nobel. Activities in the park include camping, swimming, boating, cycling and fishing. The park's proximity to southern Ontario make it very popular, especially in peak season, and reservations are often necessary despite its large number of campsites.

# 杀熊

射手张弓杀天熊，血洒长空落海滨。

白云依依绕长岸，红石殷殷照天心。

熊死魂魄成妖精，夜卷秋风啸山林。

帐外残羹吞食尽，乘云挟雾归苍冥。

# Killbear

Once upon a time, there was a war between the stars of Shooter and Bear.

The bear was shot. Along the shore, his blood was splashed over there.

Rows of white clouds as his endless grudge surround the beach and gare.

The bloody stone like his unwilling heart is just in the glare.

His spirit was so stubborn that he finally became a bogy to do dare.

In dark night, he incurs wind and sweeps through the mountains everywhere.

Furtive searching around tents, he enjoys the delicious left in dishware.

In cloud and frost he retires to the nether left his roars sound so scare.

# 山雨

罗帐系枫荫，晚来暮色青。

夜雨千重翠，秋风万木声。

天远海涛静，月小清辉明。

明朝入山径，空翠气更清。

# Rain in Forest

In maple shadows, it is my blue tent.

When dusk falling, it looks so smart.

In raining night, hundreds mountains get more verdant.

As wind blowing, thousand trees bluster hard in forest.

The vast sky is spacious while the sea is quiet.

Moon is so small but the shining is just bright.

Tomorrow I would walk in woods along the route.

After rain, the fresh mist would wet my worn coat.

# 山行

山石如幻彩，螺纹相叠排。

莘确入幽径，嶙峋出青苔。

草浅蛙隐匿，林深鹿徘徊。

灵芝生石下，慧心可采摘。

# Going Trail

In forest, the unique stones are so miraculous.

The graceful veins are overlapped in regular rows.

Ruggedly, they line up so long as a narrow path.

Irregularly, they are covered with green mosses.

Grasses on way are superficial but tiny frog hides.

Forest around is deep as deer is walking in trees.

Glossy ganoderma quietly grows near the stones,

who being intelligent could pick it up in hands.

# 听雨

枫林寂寂罗帐青，

山雨淙淙夜叩门。

帐中斜卧人不寐，

闲听穿林打叶声。

# Listening to Rain

Under the green maples, our blue tent is set up.

In dark night, rains continuously tap it on the top.

Lying down in tent, I can not get into sleep.

Then I listen to rain passing leaves drop by drop.

# 三万群岛

　　三万群岛是乔治亚湾国家公园的代表景点。景点需要坐船进行游览，在这里你可以观赏到特殊的地貌，多样的物种，以及 5000 年前的文化历史。

# 30000 Islands

The 30,000 islands, it is at Georgian Bay Islands National Park that you will discover spectacular landscapes, time-worn rock faces, diverse habitats, the rugged beauty of the Canadian Shield and cultural history dating back 5,000 years.

# 游三万群岛

海云空濛欲何行，若乘仙槎游苍穹。

一天银汉波灿烂，三万星辰碧玲珑。

水流湾環星罗布，长风瀚漫鸟翔云。

天门洞开虹桥断，汽笛一声回休仑。

# Travelling 30000 Islands

Drizzly clouds cover the sea, where will you go at present?

Oh, we seem as beginning a trip on vast sky by a fairy raft.

Brilliant ripples in the galaxy are incomparably magnificent.

The thirty thousands stars are all verdant and exquisite.

Silvery River tortuously surrounds the stars scattering apart.

Vast winds bluster hard but flying bird is close up to my chest.

As if gate of heaven being open, rainbow bridge starts to rotate.

In ringing of an air siren, Lake Huron comes back into my sight.

# 基拉尼省级公园

　　基拉尼是安大略省最受喜爱的野外活动目的地之一。其宝蓝色的湖面、白色石英岩的山脊，被认为是安大略公园系统中王冠上的明珠之一。距多伦多约 5 小时的车程。

# Killarney Provincial Park

Killarney Provincial Park is one of Ontario's the most popular wilderness destinations. With its sapphire blue lakes and white quartzite ridges it is considered one of the crown jewels of the Ontario Park system. 5 hours drive from Toronto.

# 海石

苍云吞海海未枯，老松穿石石已烂。

石烂表里俱鲜艳，殷殷赤色如血染。

红石高下岩花淡，长云舒卷海波远。

蹇足难行崎岖径，扶杖趔趄步深浅。

# Stones by Sea

Thick clouds are so wide that the sea is almost swallowed.

Old pines are so indomitable that the stones are pierced.

Broken stones emerge the bright-colored surface and inside.

They are all fresh red just like being dyed by blood.

Moss is light green on surface while red stones are rugged.

As the vast sea waves, the wide clouds roll and spread.

My sprained feet can not walk well along the hillside.

With a pine staff, I walk slowly and toddle so hard.

# 行舟

青崖与红岩，澹然一水连。

展臂深切浪，挥棹起碧澜。

乘风入荷荡，穿湖过小湾。

归来人极倦，鼾声动秋山。

# Paddling Canoe

Red cliffs and black rocks stand facing each other.

Between them, a blue lake ripples crystal water.

Widely spreading arms, we deeply paddle along the river.

Wielding paddles, our canoe is so brisk as ripples waver.

By breeze, we get into a lotus lake and smell the flower.

Passing through lake, canoe go around a small corner.

When we return, it is so much tired for each traveler.

In sleeping, we snore aloud as if hills around being in shiver.

# 荷花潭

千松岗上立，万荷潭中生。

水同松色翠，荷与月样清。

凉风拂蒻草，秋水荡浮萍。

行舟入幽境，微浪惊鱼鹰。

# Freeland Lake

Hundreds pines standing on hills around.

Thousands lotus  blooming in quiet pond.

Crystal water is so green like pines under the cloud.

Pure lotus are so clean just as moon with no shade.

Soft flags are slowly blown by the cool wind.

Slight ripples gently sway bundles of duckweed.

Although my canoe slips into here with no sound,

the cormorants are so alert that they're still disturbed.

# 基拉尼湖

天阔水远碧悠悠，湖静风凉欲晚秋。

松山映水千幢秀，红石伏波两卧牛。

行舟十里人已倦，湖湾九转不见头。

转舷趁晚且归去，来年枫红可重游。

# Killarney Lake

Endless water melts into the vast sky, they are so clear and blue.

Breeze blows over the crystal lake, they are quietly cool.

Pines standing on hills, water ripples the overlaps of graceful shadow.

Red stones stay in water, just like two oxen sleeping in river flow.

We are so tired, because more than ten miles we have paddled through.

Although corner and corner we go around, where is the end we don't know.

Dusk is approaching, we'd better go back and then turn around the bow.

In the next late autumn, we'd like trace back to enjoy this view.

# 晚宿

红崖顶上枫林静，

青石湾里秋水冷。

晚来凉风穿林过，

三五榛果落帐顶。

# Camping in Evening

Dense forest around, trees on the red cliff is quietly calm.

Black stony bay surrounds, cool water ripples in the stream.

When evening wind blows through the pines and maple.

Some autumn nuts sporadically beat my tent on the top.

# 秋晚归舟

海阔乌云压，

天高树欲拔。

归舟纤似月，

秋草细如发。

# Canoe in Retiring

Heavy cloud  presses vast sea so firmly in my eye.

Green tall trees seem to be drawn so high.

Canoe in retiring is so slim just as new moon in sky.

Small grass in fall is so tiny just as hair of guy.

097

# 西潭

　　西潭位于胭脂河的末端西侧，紧邻安大略湖。无论是春天嫩绿的垂柳，炎夏满塘的荷花，还是深秋艳丽的红蓼，都是不得不赏的美景。小小西潭，让人无限留恋。

# Xitan Pond　(Rouge River Park)

Xitan pond is located at the west side of the end of rouge river, closely up to the Lake Ontario. Whatever the verdant willows in spring or lotus in summer, or the red knotweeds in autumn, they are so charming that my heart is seized deeply.

# 西潭携友赏荷

赠君一塘芙蓉影，再加十里凉荷风。

寂寂天涯凭谁问，耿耿此心有君听。

雪藕入泥真忍辱，清荷出水素无尘。

半生辛勤且放下，暂听碧叶摇西风。

# Enjoying Lotus with a Friend in Xitan

Dear friend, send you a whole pond of lotus shadow,

besides, add ten miles of  lotus smell to you.

In this remote corner, who would concern where I solo go?

Except you, who could know what I persistently do?

Enduring the dirt in mire, the snowy roots silently grow.

Blooming out of the water, icy lotus are quietly pure.

Put down all the painstaking in half lifetime we past through.

In the trees, please listen to the lively whistle as winds blow.

# 荷塘雅趣

## 其一

白莲开时净如雪，碧叶莲塘与天接。

鹅游塘中久不去，自与荷花比皎洁。

# Spirits in Lotus Pond

## Chapter 1

When white lotus bloom, they are as pure as snow.

Joining in sky, the green leaves are floating on river's flow.

A swan is swimming in the water, not looking to go.

He is wondering whether himself or the lotus is more pure.

# 荷塘雅趣

## 其二

两三芦雁下荷塘，藕花深处嬉戏忙。

振羽摇翎不沾水，却染一身荷花香。

# Spirits in Lotus Pond

## Chapter 2

Several geese fly into the lotus pond and swim on the ripples.

Surrounded by the lotus, they are busy in playing with.

They are wantonly flapping wings but water can't wet their feathers.

However, they are so thoroughly influenced by the fragrant lotus smells.

105

# 荷塘雅趣

## 其三

红日当空小塘晴，藕花出水荷风清。

群鱼倏然桥边过，鳞光万点似流萤。

# Spirits in Lotus Pond

## Chapter 3

What a sunny day! Red sun is glowing high in sky.

Pure lotus bloom out of water as breeze blows by.

Suddenly, a ball of numerous fish floats up along the shoreline.

Passing bridge, the scales shining look as thousands points of firefly.

# 荷塘雅趣

## 其四

荷香淡淡日西沉，藕花入水晚塘清。

燕子往来总寻觅，凌波可见不可亲。

# Spirits in Lotus Pond

## Chapter 4

Sun sinks down and lotus pond suffuses the delicate fragrance.

Lotus flower shrink back into water and the pond is so grace.

Around the pond, the swallows fly over the clear ripples.

It wonders that: they are so clear in water why I can't kiss.

# 晚塘

天心寂湛妙如虹，

映出晚塘千叶金。

收却一天云霞去，

于微密处现光明。

# Lotus Pond in Summer Evening

Pure as rainbow, the Universe's soul is so miraculous.

Magically it varies out thousands gold leaves of lotus.

Generally it fades a whole sky of luster and clouds.

Secretly it demonstrates the brilliance in the tiny place.

# 西潭晚秋

枫红褪尽海波平，芦花如雪碧潭清。

寒鹭已去鸥还在，秋河半落鱼浅行。

白鸥凫波千颗玉，落霞映水满塘金。

秋云渐深人不去，霜华如梦湿晚襟。

# Late Autumn of Xitan Pond

Red leaves entirely fall away but the vast sea is smooth.

Reed flowers fly as snow while pond is in peace.

Herons have gone but gulls stay in cold winds.

River is half-dried as fish are swimming in shallow ripples.

White gulls resting on water look as thousands pure pearls.

Sunset shining spreads brilliant gold all over the pond and hills.

I'm so lured that I lost the way back in evening clouds,

although dreamlike frost diffusing in air wets my clothes.

113

# 秋鸥捕鱼图

潭静山影重，水落秋鱼丰。

鳞动千鸥聚，羽展一天擎。

凌波寻潜遁，击水捕银纹。

往来多所获，吟鸣翔碧空。

# Picture of Gulls Catching Fish in Late Fall

Shadows of blue hills are quiet in clean pond.

Fishes are abundant as river is half-dried.

The silvery leaping attracts so many gulls coming around.

Numberless pure wings spread out in sky just as white cloud.

Flying over ripples, gulls gaze at the fish attempting to hide.

Rushing into the water, they rapidly seize the fish they aimed.

After several sally, they captured adequate delicious food.

Then they freely fly in blue sky with joyful crying aloud.

115

# 秋潭

临水一簇枫叶红，

莹莹透出谁家灯？

邀君晚来赏秋色，

芦花落水悄无声。

# Autumn Pond

By the river a group of red maples are so smart,

in which whose lamp shining is so bright?

Dear friend, please enjoy the view with me despite it is so late.

Though reed flowers are falling on water, night is still silent

# 西潭秋鹭

## 其一

碧潭幽幽静水流，

浮云霭霭晚来收。

白鹭一只栖芦荡，

素羽黄纶立清秋。

# Autumn Heron in Xitan Pond

## Chapter 1

What a peaceful pond, its clean water is quietly flowing.

Slight clouds are slowly floating away in autumn evening.

Near the reeds, a white heron is lonely standing.

In clear autumn, its pure feather and yellow beak are so eye-catching.

119

# 西潭秋鹭

## 其二

山明水净芦荻青，天淡云闲秋叶红。

长雁乘风下荷荡，白鹭出水上晴空。

# Autumn Heron in Xitan Pond

## Chapter 2

Clean hills and clear water around, reeds are still green.

Clouds floating in blue sky, a bit red leaves just can be seen.

By fair wind, geese fly down  in pond as reeds are ruffling.

While herons fly up into clear sky out of river flowing.

# 西潭秋鹭

## 其三

暮霭落青山，

云水浸远天。

秋潭宿双鹭，

白羽舞翩翩。

# Autumn Heron in Xitan Pond

## Chapter3

Evening mist envelops blue hills around.

In the far, water soaks the sky and cloud.

Two herons are standing in the middle of the pond.

Suddenly, they spread pure wings, dance lightly in wind.

123

# 西潭秋鹭

## 其四

十亩绿波千层叠，藕花落去留碧叶。

白鹭飞来与鹅立，一潭翡翠三点雪。

# Autumn Heron in Xitan Pond

## Chapter 4

Ten hectares of clean water ripple layer by layer.

Lotus fall down only green leaves sway there.

A white heron comes and stays with two swans here,

just like tree points of snow dropping in a jade dishware.

# 西潭夏晚

万道毫光透浓云，

一团乌金坠波心。

扁舟一叶出芦荡，

随波载去万两金。

# Summer Evening of Xitan

Thousands beams of sharp sunlight pass through heavy cloud.

A mass of black gold falls down into the middle of the pond.

Suddenly, a leaf of canoe goes out of the ruffling reed.

It freely ripplles away with all the golden sunshine in its hold.

# 西潭秋月

秋山苍翠秋水平，

海云初起海潮生。

凭栏遥望天远静，

一轮明月照海清。

# Autumn Moon in Xitan

In early autumn, hills are verdant while water is smooth.

With oceanic tide, clouds just appear from the distance.

Beyond the rail, clear sky is in deep silence.

Round moon purifies vast sea is so clean just as crystal glass

# 西潭日出

云静天远海波舒，霞光渐由海中出。

丹霞红极展凰翼，金波亮透吐龙珠。

冉冉一颗升云际，灼灼万方天地苏。

腾入苍穹渺不见，重开秋澄天净图。

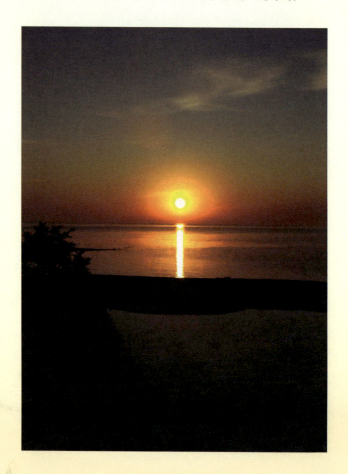

# Sunrise of Xitan

Under the sky, vast sea spreads calmly with cloud drifting away.

From sea, reddish luster slowly appears with brilliant ray.

Turning to the reddest, luster spreads phoenix's wings on the bay.

Getting to the goldest, waves gush dragon's pearl out of the sea.

Red sun slowly rises in clouds, with glaring shining it is so free.

Everything on earth is being aroused by the sunny key.

Finally, it gets into so deep space that I cann't see.

But a scroll of clear autumn and clean sky is opened in a new day.

# 西潭邀友望月

六月十四夜抒怀，西潭邀友望月来。

海天一轮转玉镜，碧霄千顷光华开。

月下荷芰凌水净，光中燕鸥浴雪白。

水天俱与人澄澈，素辉莹莹满襟怀。

# Enjoying the Moon Rising in Xitan with Friends

In evening of June 14, I gathered some old friends together.

As freely expressing our minds, we enjoyed the full moon to appear.

Out of sea, a round moon looked like a bright rising mirror.

In the vast blue sky, glittering moonbeams began to luster.

Above clear water, a snowy moonlight purifies the lotus flower.

Flying in sky, gulls and swallows seemed as in diffusing silver.

The glittering moonlight clarifies everything between the sky and water.

I, myself was purged so thoroughly just as in a clean shower.

133

# 西潭落日

长风拂云暮色远，夕阳晚晖碧草连。

朱霞天半染绿树，红珠一颗落青山。

云里泼金光灿烂，水中燃火波炫然。

鸥燕翻飞云渐落，丹霞流彩映水天。

# Sunset of Xitan

Winds from far blow through the vast clouds.

Sunset shining widely spreads all over the grasses

Pink luster reddens all the green trees.

A red pearl falls down into the blue hills.

As if gold splashing in clouds, the sky is so glorious.

Just like fire burning in water, ripples get so lustrous.

Sun disappears but gulls and swallows are flying in winds.

Brilliant twilight remains in the sky and ripples.

# 西潭春晚

云容天净起海头，冰河渐开溪细流。

红蓼褪尽青芦长，白雪消半绿鸯游。

日落林表千层秀，月照春波一潭幽。

满怀心事何人诉，夜凉春鸟鸣啁啾。

# Spring Evening in Xitan

Leisurely clouds are floating to the end of sky and sea.

Frozen river just thaws it flows in a narrow way.

Red knotweeds fall away but reeds are just green.

White snow is thawing and swimming ducks are so free.

On treetops, sunset spreads overlaps of graceful ray.

In moonlight, a whole pond appears quiet and pale.

So many worries in my heart. Who can I say?

In cool evening, spring birds are crying from where they stay.

137

# 西潭春日

## 其一

毕竟西潭春色好，东风一吹便灵妙。

细柳拂堤摇曳曳，小荷点水绿渺渺。

云阴潭静春水涨，草新芦青野鸳到。

海平天净风正暖，同君凭栏作远眺。

138

# Spring View in Xitan

## Chapter 1

After all, spring view in Xitan is just charming.

When spring wind blows, it becomes a lovely painting.

Along the bank, willow sprays are slightly swaying and swaying.

On the water, tiny leaves of lotus are gently rippling and rippling.

In cloudy days, the pond is quiet while the water is slowly rising.

As geese and ducks come back, grasses are tender and reeds turn green.

Facing smooth sea, wind blows gently and the warm sun is shining.

On so nice day, we should stay on the deck and enjoy the lively living.

# 西潭春日

## 其二

春莺乱啼谷雨天，

绿柳鹅黄淡如烟。

胭脂水涨碧潭静，

芦芽参差野鸥还。

# Spring View in Xitan

## Chapter 2

Clever birds are freely singing in later spring sky.

Green willows are just light yellow as if dim mist in my eye.

Clean pond is so quiet while water rises above the former shoreline.

Irregular reed shoots are brand new as wild gulls just retire.

# 西潭春日

## 其三

青枫湾里飞白羽，

水空澹澹风煦煦。

可人最是西潭水，

深是靛蓝浅是绿。

# Spring View in Xitan

## Chapter 3

In the bay, birds are flying and maples are green a little.

Blue sky is so pure while breezes gently blow.

Only spring water here could ripple my soul.

Because the shallow is green while the deep is indigo.

143

# 游三河口贺故友生日

春花渐老夏木阴，贺君新岁登翠峰。

一谷清风拂人静，两溪绿水绕山青。

涧花落蝶蝶灿烂，山石分水水淙泷。

今日祝君当何似，身似青山心如云。

# Celebrating a Friend's Birthday at the Delta

Spring flowers fall down and the lush trees prop up wide shades.

Climbing up the hill, we celebrate your birthday in cool breeze.

Breeze blowing through, the whole valley is just in silence.

Surrounding the hill, two streams flow quietly with clean ripples.

Butterfly rests on the blooming tree, it reveals its brilliance.

River bypasses the stone in water, it still sings its clear sounds.

Dear friend, how can I bless you at the date of your birth?

I bless your body is strong as blue hill and heart is free as white clouds.

# 西潭立秋赏月

云影天光碧水澄，西潭秋来似画屏。

枫柳荷塘一色翠，水天月色两泓金。

夏暑才消人初静，秋凉渐长气方清。

闲歌惊起芦中雁，云外传来三两声。

# Enjoying Moon in Xitan at Beginning of Autumn

Blue sky and floating cloud are reflected in the clean pond.

Today, beautiful Xitan is like a screen being elegantly painted.

Maples, willows and lotus are all as identically verdant as green jade.

Moon in sky and the shadow in water seem as two rounds of glittering gold.

I just feel a bit crisp while summer hot is slightly relieved.

Autumn cool slowly appears as air in nature is to be purified.

My free singing frightens the geese in the reed.

They fly into the sky and scattered cries sound from the cloud.

147

# 西潭秋晚

秋云如梦锁碧潭，枫清柳静藕花残。

燕子飞去巢空在，野鸥萍聚秋水寒。

云衔红日欲西坠，水映白鹭飞长天。

一年好景今将去，襟衫轻寒泪莫沾。

# Autumn Evening in Xitan

Dreamlike clouds are covering the clear pond.

Maples and willows are standing quietly but lotuses are withered.

Swallows have gone but their empty nests are unchanged.

Wild gulls stay together while water in autumn gets cold.

Red sunset shining is faint as if being held by the thick cloud.

Clean water reflects the flying heron is so refined.

Autumn in coming will bring down everything I admired.

My unlined garment is too thin to bear the cold with my sad.

# 西潭冬夜

冰轻半塘连，雪净芦花残。

天黑归寒雁，灯红映碧潭。

叶落山影静，鸟宿水云喧。

夜凉当归去，吟歌与君还。

# Winter Night in Xitan

Almost covering half pond, the ice is slight and thin.

Reeds are withered while snow is just clean.

As dusk falling, geese are coming back for resting.

In clear water, the reflections of lamps are shining.

Leaves fallen, shadows of hills are quietly riffling.

Mists diffusing, lodging birds are still crying.

Heavily cold around us, it reminds our retiring.

In the cloudy way back, there is only our clear sing.

# 冬潭

寒潭已冰封，晚霞尚余空。

天清一轮月，山静半塘风。

云幻霓虹彩，水化琉璃青。

芦中鸥雁去，归来应到春。

# Winter Pond

Cold winter coming, the whole pond gets freezing.

As dusk falling, brilliant twilight remains charming.

In blue sky, a round clean moon is brightly glowing.

Quiet hills around half pond, cold wind is blowing.

Iridescent cloud just as rosy silk is so fine and dazzling.

Frozen pond as if dark green lazurite is smooth and clean.

Reeds are withered, where no gulls and geese can be seen.

When they come back, maybe it is the next spring.

153

# 三河口

枫绒碧草幽壑生，清流宛转入深松。

双溪汇成胭脂水，孤山染出翡翠峰。

鸟啼百啭黄山雀，花开三瓣素延龄。

寂寂春岭罕人至，穿花绕石且徐行。

# Delta

In quiet valley, flowering maples and green grasses seem as spring dream .

Flowing into deep verdant pines, the clean creek is quietly calm.

Two streams converge together, they become rouge river downstream.

Greened by spring trees, the jade-like mountain appear so charm.

Chirping happily, the yellow birds are just in free game.

Blooming out three petals, there is a large piece of trillium.

In this remote mountains, the travelers are absolutely seldom.

Passing by flowers and going around rocks, only you and I slowly move.

155

# 汤米·汤普森公园

　　汤米·汤普森公园位于多伦多湖滨，距市中心只有几分钟的路程，是一个独特的城市野生公园。该园区位于一个叫做莱斯利街沙嘴的人造半岛上，其延伸到安大略湖内 5 公里，有超过 500 公顷面积。公园代表了一些现存最大的多伦多湖滨地区的自然栖息地。大片野花草地、卡顿树林、湖滨沼泽、鹅卵石海滩和沙丘仅是汤米·汤普森公园中的一部分动植物栖息地。野生动物，尤其鸟类，在园区兴旺地繁衍。此公园在大多地区( GTA )为人们提供了一个观察自然的最好的地方。

# Tommy Thompson Park

Located on the Toronto waterfront, Tommy Thompson Park is a unique urban wilderness minutes from downtown. The park is located on a man-made peninsula, known as the Leslie Street Spit, which extends five kilometers into Lake Ontario and is over 500 hectares in size. The park represents some of the largest existing natural habitat on the Toronto waterfront. Wildflower meadows, cottonwood forests, coastal marshes, cobble beaches and sand dunes are just some of the habitats at Tommy Thompson Park. Wildlife, especially birds, flourishes at the park, which provides one of the best nature watching areas in the GTA.

# 湖滨晚景

彩霞如火海波蓝，草树拂堤鸥鹭还。

长岬湾環十里远，广厦层鳞一水连。

百鸟归林云霞静，一塔参天世界宽。

天阔水远渺无际，春风荡漾动春衫。

# Evening View of Lakeshore

Blue sea is quiet and the sunset shining is aflame.

Trees are swaying on the bank as herons and gulls come.

A ten miles cape extends in water just like a bending arm.

By the water, great mansions stand there team upon team.

Hundreds birds retired in forest and the charming twilight is calm.

The CN tower stands high in sky, it widens people's view and life.

Sea and sky are so vast, my sight can not reach the extreme.

In spring wind rippling, my shirt is just like a spring wave.

# 湖滨夜景

海色天容俱碧蓝，蜃景飘渺现云间。

千幢华彩立长岸，一塔玲珑照海天。

云霞十里渐远淡，星火万点正莹然。

粼粼波光映何处？彩鸳夜归动春涟。

# Night View of Lakeshore

Whatever the sky or sea, they are so blue at all.

Emerging out of clouds, the charming scenery is like a dreamful scroll.

What a gorgeous view! Numerous brilliant mansions stand on the lakeshore.

Lightening the sky and sea, the exquisite tower is incomparably tall.

Scattering about ten miles away, twilight and clouds begin to fall.

A myriad twinkling lights are shining, the whole city is so peaceful.

On the glittering water, why are the ripples getting more and more?

Oh, there is a couple of mandarin ducks coming from their tour.

# 湖滨观鸟

湖滨山水胜，百鸟宿春林。

巢浅栖夜鹭，树高立鱼鹰。

千鸥聚沙岸，白鹭飞长空。

鸳鸯双戏水，款款渡春风。

# Observing Birds on Lakeshore

Along the lakeside, there are so wonderful views.

Numerous birds set their nests on the green trees.

In the small nests, night herons stay in silence.

On the treetops, fish hawks gather together with noises.

All over the lakeshore, there are thousands sea gulls.

While a white heron is flying so high in blue space.

A couple of mandarin ducks are playing happily on the ripples.

In spring winds, they are enjoying the admirable time.

# 湖滨观焰火

海天霹雳鸣，烛花耀苍穹。

流星万点雨，火树一天明。

映空霓虹散，照水落星辰。

华彩倏寂灭，云烟尚飘空。

# Enjoying Fireworks on Lakeshore

Between sky and sea, we suddenly hear thunderclaps.

In the air, there appear gorgeous fireworks.

So many splendid shooting stars look as lustrous rains.

In blue sky, the aflame trees widely spread brilliance.

Shining the sky, they are just like broken rainbows.

Lightening the water, they appear as falling stars.

Suddenly, all the magnificence ends in silence.

Only cloud and smoke are flying in empty space.

165

# 莫宁塞公园

  莫宁塞公园位于多伦多市士嘉堡地区，是一个地区级公园。公园占踞了高地河的大部分深谷，拥有 416.7 英亩（1.686 平方公里）的面积。公园东接莫宁塞大道、北临额斯美路、南边与劳伦斯大道东道相接。公园与莫宁塞大道东边的多伦多大学士嘉堡分校一起，沿着高地河的下流形成了一个连续的绿化带。和多伦多的其它公园相比，这个公园有着以鹿、风蚀的悬崖和残余的树林组成的较高级别的城市野生环境的特点。

# Morningside Park

Morningside Park is a regional park located in Scarborough, Toronto. The park occupies most of the deep valley of Highland Creek, spanning 416.7 acres (1.686 km2). The park is bounded by Morningside Avenue on the east, Ellesmere Road on the north and Lawrence Avenue East to the south. Together with the University of Toronto Scarborough lands east of Morningside Avenue, the park forms a continuous forested corridor along the lower reaches of Highland Creek. The park features a high degree of urban wilderness compared to other parks in Toronto, with deer, eroded cliffs and a remnant forest.

# 莫宁塞公园冬晚

## 其一

寂寞寒林立晚风，雪岭近在溪水滨。

半山斜绕十里路，一溪横穿百丈冰。

山鸟才去留雪印，寒叶落尽水无痕。

闲客远来不识径，两脚深浅任西东。

# Winter Evening of Morningside Park

## Chapter 1

Rows by rows, the withered trees stand there in silence.

By the stream, there are continuous snow-covered mountains.

Along the hillside, a winding narrow path extends more than ten miles.

Flowing slowly, the stream pierces through hundreds meters of ice.

Birds just fly away but they left paw prints in the white snows.

Leaves fell down entirely, in the clear water they are all traceless.

Guests from the far are not familiar with the ways.

With deep and shallow steps, their travelling is so aimless.

# 莫宁塞公园冬晚

## 其二

雪径无人山清幽，小桥临水暮云收。

山鸟含惊点水去，松鼠迎风立枝头。

古木穿堤虬根露，寒雪抱石溪绕流。

诗情却随流水去，穿峰过岭漫山游。

# Winter Evening of Morningside Park

## Chapter 2

Quiet path is snow-covered and nobody past.

Small bridge across stream, they are all melted into dusk mist.

Birds skim over the stream and fly away out of the forest.

Facing the wind, squirrels stay on the pine branches with no fret.

Old tree pierces through the impaired dike and exposes the vigorous root.

White snows nestle the stones, the stream surrounds them and flows light.

With the flowing stream, my poetic mood goes far away though it is so late.

Passing peaks and slopes, it freely roams in the valley even without foot.

# 莫宁塞公园秋日

故人何殷勤，邀我望秋红。

山色浓且淡，水流浅复深。

枫红人渐老，秋澄气全清。

拂衣且归去，江海一闲人。

# Autumn of Morningside Park

Old friend is so kind,

He invites me to find out if the maples are red.

Dusk by light alternating, mountains are under cloud.

Deep to shallow exchanging, river is flowing with no sound.

Red maple leaves tell me I'm growing old.

Clean air in autumn purifies all the world.

Swinging my worn coat, I would retire from the hard.

Between the sea and river, I should be a free man with no sad.

# 掰得烂地

　　掰得烂地位于安大略省的英格伍德（Inglewood）和切尔滕纳姆（Cheltenham）村庄附近，是一个地球科学领域中的自然与科学关注范畴（ANSI）。这一地带位于老基地线路（Old Base Line Road）南边（在安大略省10号公路和Creditview路／皮尔区12号路之间），具有裸露和侵蚀昆斯滕页岩（Queenston Shale）的特征。

# Badlands

The Badlands, near the villages of Inglewood and Cheltenham, Ontario, are an Earth Science Area of Natural and Scientific Interest (ANSI). The site is located on the south side of Old Base Line Road (between Ontario Highway 10 and Creditview Road/Peel Regional Road 12) and features exposed and eroded Queenston Shale.

# 掰得烂地

大腹坦坦向青天，红肌裸裸卧秋山。

山下红叶同我艳，天上白云如我闲。

远溯洪荒为沧海，时到今日非良田。

春花秋草均不长，日拂月照纯浩然。

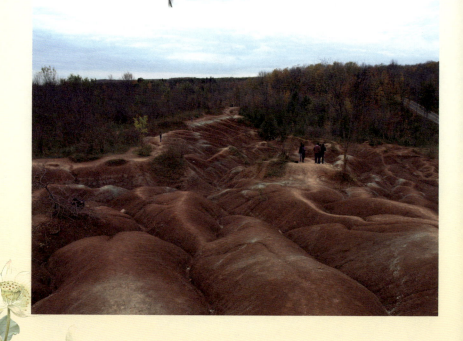

# Badlands

Naturally I show my bare abdomen under the sky.

Day by day, exposing red muscles, I never am shy.

Similar to me, maples below are also bright as red dye.

Just as me, clouds above are so free and slowly fly.

In distant memory, I was vast sea. It leaves me a deep sigh.

Today, I'm not a crop field although day by day goes by.

Neither flowers nor trees can stay here, who knows why?

Facing sun and moon, I still keep my natural features with no reply.

# 霍普港

　　霍普港是一个在加拿大安大略省南部的自辖市，位于多伦多以东 109 公里（68 公里），金斯顿以西约 159 公里（99 英里）。它坐落在安大略湖北岸的 Ganaraska 河入湖口，在诺森伯兰郡的西端。

# Port Hope

Port Hope is a municipality in Southern Ontario, Canada, about 109 kilometres (68 mi) east of Toronto and about 159 kilometres (99 mi) west of Kingston. It is located at the mouth of the Ganaraska River on the north shore of Lake Ontario, in the west end of Northumberland County.

# 三文鱼洄流

灵盈咫尺一宛然，肌碎身破不自怜。

一线洄游穿洋过，万里归心碧海悬。

江畔红叶血染就，涧底愁云气滋渲。

陌上行人不忍看，临波三叹泪潸然。

# Migration of Salmon

What a nimble arm-sized fish!

With injured body, they never mind the waves lash.

Retiring along a long route, the way back is so harsh.

Swimming through the vast sea, they keep the firm wish.

The blood lost in river, maples around are dyed reddish.

Tragic air suffuses the valley, they still strive to dash.

Travelers can't endure seeing so many lives that will vanish.

Tears trickling down, sadness substitutes their travelling pash.

# 米尔恩水坝保护区公园

　　米尔恩公园被认为是万锦市（Markham）保存最好的珍宝之一，因为它具有多种多样的植物和野生动物。每年春季和秋季，在清晨和晚上可以看到许多候鸟，在米尔恩大坝保护公园中途歇息。

# Milne Dam Conservation Park

Mine Dam Conservation Park is considered one of the best kept treasures of Markham because it features a variety of plants and wildlife. View every spring and fall,the many migratory birds in the early mornings and evenings as they stop off in Milne Dam Conservation Park.

# 湖湾小景

芦风吹波汀花开，

渔翁闲坐松荫台。

青天流云白鸥去，

红萼照水蝶飞来。

# Views of Small Lake

Along the shore, wind blows the reeds as flowers are blooming.

In the pine shadow, a fish man is blithely resting.

In blue sky, clouds are drifting and the gull is flying.

Water reflects red flowers, where the butterfly is so charming.

# 冬日

寒云垂天廓，薄日映晚霞。

水湾四五里，墟落八九家。

雪径罕人至，冰湖难藏鸭。

闲客三俩子，寥落在天涯。

# Views in Winter

In the overcast sky, there are adrift clouds.

Sunset is faint and the twilight is lusterless.

Bend of the river flows almost four or five miles,

where there scatter about eight or nine homes.

The snow-covered path is quiet and nobody passes.

On the frozen lake, duck can hardly stay.

There only scatter two or three travelers,

they are all wandering around in this remote place.

# 好愿景公园

　　好愿景公园位于 1700 多伦多市珐么丝大道 (Pharmacy Ave)。主要交叉口是珐么丝大道和 401 高速公路。是一个综合性公园，集休闲游览、儿童娱乐、文体活动与会展交流于一园。

# Wishing Well Park

Wishing well park is at 1700 Pharmacy Ave, Toronto, ON M1T 1H7. It is located at the intersection of Pharmacy Ave and 401 highway. A wide variety of both drop in and registered programs are offered for preschoolers, children, youth, adults and older adults.

# 春韵

寂寞待春人，踏雪寻芳踪。

一园冰雪净，半坡松柏新。

枝寒微芽露，雪覆幽草生。

欲知春韵到，还看苔返青。

# Spring Trace

Staying lonely, I'm waiting for spring.

Walking on snow, I want to find whether it's coming.

In the small yard, the ice and snow are so clean.

On the hillside, the old pines are still green.

In cold wind, tender shoots on tree just can be seen.

Under the thick snow, tiny grasses have been growing.

After all, I know the spring is approaching,

for the moss on the tree begins moistening.

# 红果树

碧血点点傲寒冬，

留得江山一树红。

我有丹心自红艳，

何必遥遥待春风。

# Red Fruit Tree

Disdaining the cold winter, red fruit tree shows the brave.

In the world, I'm the only scarlet left with no flower in bloom.

With faithful heart, I could turn red by myself.

Why do I have to be red after spring winds come?

# 夏晚观垒

淡金斜阳一树低，

青松绿草却依依。

闲坐凉台观垒战，

千叶枫影落人衣。

# Enjoying Softball Games in Summer Evening

The falling sun set is so lower just as the trees.

Pines and grasses are so lively in the gold rays.

Sitting on the chairs, we are enjoying the softball games.

In sun shining, so many leaves of maple shadow are printed on our clothes.

# 御马林公园

御马林公园位于窝顿大道和汉庭武大道东道的交叉口，是一处小型的社区公园。供人们休闲散步，儿童娱乐，并有网球场供大众锻炼。

# Bridlewood Park

Major intersection: Warden Ave. and Huntingwood Ave. East. A wide variety of both drop in and registered programs are offered for preschoolers, children, youth, adults and older adults.

# 春晚游园

枫径曲曲入松荫，闲坐白石听黄莺。

春鸟呖呖啼幽静，松鼠的的摇碧青。

飞泉流瀑湿童履，秋千摆翠荡红裙。

小园常来今几许？踏雪吟春已三冬。

# Evening Walking in Spring

From maples to pines, it is a winding narrow path.

Through which, I rest on white stones to hear yellow birds.

The birds are singing so happily in silence.

Squirrels stay on green pines and shake the branches.

Water from the fountains wets the kids' shoes.

On flying swings, girls are floating their red skirts.

How many times did I come to this park in past days?

Oh, stepping on snow, I met spring here three times.

# 春晚送别

霞静如绮花乱飞，

离家十年君欲归。

陌上相坐寂无语，

小月如钩淡如眉。

# Seeing a Friend off in Spring Evening

Flowers are falling and twilight looks as charming silk.

Left hometown for ten years, but now you decide to go back.

Face to face, we sit on hillside for long  with no talk.

Do you find the hooked new moon is your eyebrow alike?

# 晚归

松影斜阳映草坡，

流云如水动天波。

半推小车坡上过，

老父牵儿一路歌。

# Going Home in Evening

From pines, slightly gold sunset are shining on grasses.
Watery clouds drifting in sky, they look as layers of waves.
Slowly pushing a baby car, the father and son go forwards.
Singing on their way, they are enjoying so much happiness.

# 秋晨

枫影幢幢红日升，

小径转入青松林。

林氛轻阴将散去，

嘤嘤草虫鸣秋晨。

# Autumn Morning

Shadows of maples are luxuriant as sun rises.

A narrow path winds into the green pines.

Mists in trees are scattering when breeze blows.

In autumn morning, some insects still sing in grasses.

# 秋晴

松青菊黄似画图，

两三红叶才染出。

一片晚霞落天外，

映出树树火珊瑚。

# Sunny Autumn

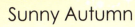

Pines are verdant and daisy is yellow in the charming fall.

A few red leaves are just dyed out in a painted scroll.

In the end of sky, the twilight is slowly passing through.

The brilliance of luster turns the trees into burning coral.

# 雪戏图

雪净莹光映天晴，

小童三五上银坪。

肚贴山脊疾飞去，

笑语盈盈似流星。

# Skiing

Glittering in sunny day, the snowy world seems as a silvery bar.

Climbing up the snowy hills, how happily the boys are.

Belly  nestling up to the hillside, they are skiing afar.

Laughing aloud, the skiing boy is just like shooting star.

209

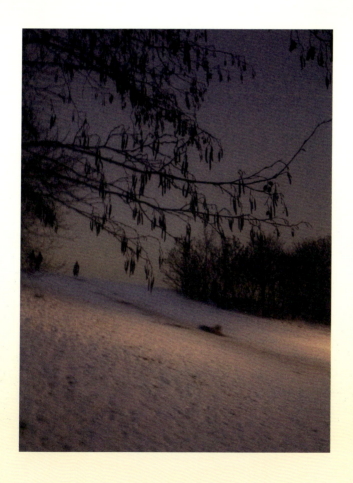

# 高园

　　高园位于多伦多 1873 号布卢尔西街（Bloor St. West)。高园是多伦多最大的公众公园，设有许多步行小道、体育设施、多样化的植被、美丽的湖畔、方便的停车、公交系统容易到达、溜狗的公园、动物园、儿童活动场地、几个餐馆、温室、野餐区，以及一群松鼠和一年四季各种各样的活动。

# High Park

High Park is located at 1873 Bloor Street West, Toronto, ON, M6S. High Park is Toronto's largest public park featuring many hiking trails, sports facilities, diverse vegetation, a beautiful lakefront, convenient parking, easy public transit access, a dog park, a zoo, playgrounds for children, a couple of eateries, greenhouses, picnic areas, a bunch of squirrels and various events throughout the year.

211

# 高园赏樱

春湾绿柳生，汀上绽红樱。

绚空千蝶胜，映水一岸云。

缤纷胜芍李，浓艳逊桃红。

花海春潮动，俱是赏花人。

# Enjoying Cherry Blossoms in High Park

In the bay, willows get green as wind is warm.

Along the shore, oriental cherries just bloom.

So brilliance in sky, thousands butterflies show the charm.

So grace on shore, shadows of pink cloud ripples in stream.

The flowers are so flourishing than peony and plum.

Their colour is a bit light than the peach blossom.

Converging into the flower sea, continuous guests still come.

Enjoying so beautiful view, everybody looms the spring dream.

213

# 春日

溪头碧波凫野鸭，水绿春草遍天涯。

千枝红樱映翠柳，一树玉兰幽谷发。

鹅游款款浮白玉，兰芷纤纤吐嫩芽。

扁舟一叶随波去，春风万里忘归家。

# Spring Day

In the river mouth, ducks are swimming on the clean water.

Spring water dyes grasses green all over the remote conner.

Beside willows, thousand branches of cherry blossoms are so luster.

In quiet valley, a tall magnolia tree is in full flower.

Leisurely swimming in water, swan is so pure as if floating silver.

Just going out of water, the sprouting flags are slight and tender.

By a brisk canoe, I would like to flow down along the river.

I'm afraid of losting the way back for the spring wind blows me so warmer.

# 美丽径公园

美丽径公园位于史刁大道上，McCowan 和米德菲之间，这是一个方便于士嘉堡和万锦市附近居民的公园。是一个综合性公园，集休闲游览、儿童娱乐、文体活动与会展交流于一园。绿树成荫、绿草如茵、花香鸟语，令人流连忘返。这个公园以放风筝活动而有名。

# Milliken Park

Milliken Park is located at the southeast corner of McCowan Road and Steeles Avenue. A wide variety of both drop in and registered programs are offered for preschoolers, children, youth, adults and older adults. These include visual arts, dance, fitness, youth leadership, drop in and instructional sports programs, a variety of camps and much more. It is famous with playing kites in spring.

# 秋晚即兴

枫径回环小路弯，微雨如丝湿袖衫。

草陂青青缓高下，芦洼浅浅泛清涟。

秋月无心空映水，老友随意同休闲。

枫叶将红人将去，归程何计却姗姗。

# Jottings in Autumn Evening

Around a circle, maples are standing and path is winding.

Tiny, silken drips wet my coat, it is merely drizzling.

Mildly alternating up and down, gentle slopes are so green.

Reeds surround the small pond, the ripples are so clean.

Full moon is shining as its shadow is plainly rippling.

Meeting together, friend and I are leisurely walking.

Maples are to be red, shall we return to hometown for an ease living?

Oh, I guess the charming views of autumn would delay your planning.

# 夏晚观锦鲤

## 其一

芦洼清浅绿水明，

青鱼团簇动鳞纹。

一丛锦鲤飘然过，

五彩流云水中生。

# Enjoying Variegated Carps in Summer Evening

## Chapter 1

Reeds are green and water is clean in summer evening.

So many black fishes are swimming in a grouping.

Graceful variegated carps are slowly passing,

as if gorgeous clouds in water just being floating.

# 夏晚观锦鲤

## 其二

红鳞如火游碧波，野鸭频追总不得。

悠然摆尾穿草去，却被灵龟亲芳泽。

# Enjoying Variegated Carps in Summer Evening

## Chapter 2

As if floating fire, the red carp is swimming in clean ripples.

A duck can't touch it although it always follows its trace.

Shaking tail leisurely, the red carp passes by the waterweeds.

Unfortunately, it is kissed by a clever tortoise.

# 夏晚观锦鲤

## 其三

五彩锦鳞何绚然，碧波荡漾起斑斓。

忽来倏去频聚散，流光画出太极环。

# Enjoying Variegated Carps in Summer Evening

## Chapter 3

What a variegated carp! They swim blithely in team and row.

Their gorgeous running trace swings out ripple and ripple.

Quick gathering and sudden scattering, they freely come and go.

Magically, their florid swimming trace draws out a Taiji circle.

# 爱德华花园

　　爱德华花园位于多伦多植物园旁，在莱斯利街和劳伦斯大道的拐角上。这个以前的庄园花园在高坡上种有多年生植物和玫瑰，在凹处有野花、杜鹃花和大量的假山。在凹处较上层，孩子们的教学花园旁，还有一个可爱的植物园。

# Edwards Garden

Edwards Garden sits adjacent to the Toronto Botanical Garden, at the corner of Leslie Street and Lawrence Avenue. This former estate garden features perennials and roses on the uplands and wildflowers, rhododendrons and an extensive rockery in the valley. On the upper level of the valley there is also a lovely arboretum beside the children's Teaching Garden.

227

# 秋日送友人

暮晚入秋壑，邀友望枫红。

风摇万点火，雨落一地金。

人随路宛转，山任水纵横。

红叶半零落，天涯别故人。

# Seeing a Friend off in Autumn

In evening, I come into the valley with my friend.

To see him off, we together enjoy maples just being in red.

Red leaves look like thousands pieces of fire shivering in wind.

After rain, fallen leaves seem as bright gold all over the ground.

In our life, we always have to run along the complicated road,

just as the river always flows along the intricate hillside.

At this movement, the maples leaves become half-withered.

From now on, you and I will be remotely separated.

229

# 法兰西河省级公园

　　法兰西河省级公园位于多伦多北部大约 2.5 小时车程。毗邻基拉尼省级公园，碧蓝的法兰西河缓缓流过，两岸苍翠的松树和枫树林立，是野营和划船以及秋季赏枫叶的好去处。

# French River Provincial Park

French river Provincial Park is just 2.5 hours drive north of Toronto, closely up to Killarney Provincial Park. Purely blue river slowly flows away, along both bank, verdant pines and maples quietly stand there. It is a good place for camping, paddling and enjoying red leaves in autumn.

# 秋河

青翠两岸松，

秋水一湾明。

人家住何处，

簇簇红叶中。

# French River in Autumn

Along the both banks, there are flourishing pines.

Flowing through the small bend, the water glitters

In this late autumn, where are the households?

Oh, in the group of red maples, you can find their homes.

# 悬崖公园

　　悬崖公园有很长的沙滩、野餐区、散步小路，和了望台。它位于士嘉堡悬崖的下方，由 5000 年历史的结实粘土因风蚀而形成的悬崖。车辆可以沿着 Brimley 路向南行驶到它的终点，进入悬崖公园。也可以坐公交车到达。

# Bluffer's Park

Bluffer's Park has a long sandy beach, picnic areas, walks, and lookouts. It is located beneath the Scarborough Bluffs, a 5000 year-old escarpment formed by the erosion of packed clay. Vehicles can enter Bluffer's Park by traveling south on Brimley Road to its end point. It also can be reached by public transit.

# 悬崖公园

## 其一

春湾清且浅，海澄天湛然。

水廊依长岸，崖壁立海天。

鸟去水空静，人来林树喧。

谁家生炊火，青霭绕春山。

# Bluffer's Park

# Chapter 1

What a clearly shallow bay!

Blue sky and clean sea are all in sunny ray.

Along the long lakeside, it is a surrounding veranda way.

Under the blue sky, the steep cliff is facing the sea.

The bay is so silent after birds fly away.

The forest is so racket when persons stay.

In verdant mountains, who are enjoy barbecue in spring day?

Enchanting smell is flying in air, swaying a wisp of slight gray.

237

# 悬崖公园

## 其二

春山雨初住，沙径纤无尘。

海澄平似镜，崖青净如屏。

鸟啼水色里，人行枫影中。

极目海天远，随意作长吟。

238

# Bluffer's Park

## Chapter 2

Spring in mountains, it rained last night.

Along beach, sandy path was washed with no dust.

Clean sea like smooth mirror is blue and vast.

Steep cliff as a screen is straight and bright.

Crying birds are flying with clear reflections in water.

People is walking in overlapping shadows of maple forest.

Looking into far, sky and sea extend all over my sight.

Singing freely, so graceful views pleasure my spirit.

# 悬崖公园

## 其三

天晚海霞生，日落断崖阴。

水同天青绿，霞若胭脂红。

澄波舒千里，春月淡无痕。

兴来邀朋子，临海望月行。

# Bluffer's Park

## Chapter 3

In spring evening, the sunset glow slowly appears.

From sea, it is so lustrous as cliff is in shadows.

Water is so clean just as celestine-coloured glass.

Sky is so bright as if being in rouge-like redness.

The vast sea spreads widely over thousand miles.

The faint moon hangs high and it is almost traceless

In light mood, I invite my friend to enjoy the views.

Along the sea, we slowly walk under the moonbeams.

241

# 东点公园

　　东点公园是一个 60 公顷面积的公园，在安大略湖北岸，劳伦斯大道东道以南，莫宁塞大道以东。它是观鸟和赏蝶的好去处。

# East-point Park

East Point Park is a 60 hectares park on the north shore of Lake Ontario, south of Lawrence Ave East and east of Morningside Ave. It's a good place to bird-watching and butterfly-watching.

# 安湖河口

海平微风静，天阔白云轻。

鸥翔千里外，风荡一怀中。

环堤绕山走，长岬劈海行。

临风望日落，碧水照人清。

244

# River Mouth to Lake Ontario

Over the smooth sea, the breeze is so quiet.

Drifting in vast sky, white clouds are so light.

Going hundreds miles away, gulls fly so fast.

Surrounding in my chest, the wind is so smart.

A narrow meandering goes along the piedmont.

Extending in sea, the stony banks are straight.

With cool breeze, we enjoy the charming sunset.

In clear water, our shadows are floating about.

245

# 暑日山行

岬外日烈烈，壑中风习习。

山幽鸟声脆，水清鱼现脊。

林阴光欲断，草深路渐稀。

山溪将尽处，豁然海天曦。

# Valley Hiking in Midsummer

Out of the valley, sun shining is hotter and hotter.

Getting into the valley, breeze is cooler and cooler.

Hills around are so quiet, birds-singing sounds clearer.

Small river is so clean, fish's back appears distincter.

Trees are so dense that sun shining gets fainter.

Grasses are so deep that the trail becomes rarer.

The river flows down where it seems to disappear.

Suddenly, vast sea and sky appear and sun shining is brighter.

# 於人村

於人村是万锦市的一个郊区村庄。它离多伦多市中心
33 公里，在富豪山庄南部以东 4 公里。 於人村最初建于
1794 年。红河从於人村中央部分的北部流向其东南部。当
地被保护地带的步行道可以直接连通到村里的大道上，其中
最常用的是土沽塘周围的步行道。历史上的村庄，或着说於
人村中心部分是一个典型的小镇，其发展从 19 世纪 40 年代
初到 20 世纪中后期，大约经历了一个多世纪左右的时间。
历史悠久的於人村主街每年吸引成千上万的游客。

# Unionville

Unionville is a suburban village in Markham. It is located 33 km northeast of downtown Toronto and 4 km east of southern Richmond Hill. Unionville originally was founded in 1794. Rouge River runs north of the central part of Unionville and to the southeast. Walking paths through the local conservation lands connect directly to the village roads, one of the most used being the path around Toogood Pond. The historic village or downtown section of Unionville is typical of a small town that developed over a century or so starting in the early 1840s through the middle to late 20th century. The historic Main Street Unionville attracts thousands of visitors each year.

249

# 秋望

芦花随水远，秋河一天开。

菊香桑陌静，雁啼霜风来。

命同天地大，身共草木衰。

登台临水望，一生几徘徊？

# Autumn View

Reeds are so flourishing as far as the flowing water.

Beginning from the end of sky, it is just Rouge River.

Mulberries quietly stand in the field with daisy flower.

Geese crying in frost wind, it turns cooler and cooler.

My spirit like the entire Universe is undying for ever.

My body as plants in fall will wither sooner or later.

Standing on the platform, looking far in cloudy weather,

In my life, how many times is my heart in shiver?

# 秋塘

枫红柳叶黄，芦花随风扬。

微雨明霁色，秋水映斜阳。

白鸥落青闸，苍鹭栖池塘。

绿鸭正凫水，粼粼动波光。

# Autumn Pond

Maples' leaves get red and willows' became yellow.

In cool winds, reed flowers adrift fly through.

Drizzling stopped, it clears up and sun shining begins to show.

In sunset shining, autumn pond is so clean and pure.

White gulls stay on black sluice while river flows below.

A heron rests in reeds and the water ripples its shadow.

On the clear pond, green ducks are swimming slow.

Layers by layers, the glittering ripples gently glow.

253

# 暮鸭

## 其一

秋塘柳依依，

野鸭正凫水。

夜凉何处去？

穿塘入芦苇。

254

# Ducks in Dusk

## Chapter 1

Wickers are quietly swaying along the lakeside.

Wild ducks are slowly swimming in the pond.

As dusk falling, where will they go in cold wind?

Oh, they pass through the pond and then rest in the reed.

255

# 暮鸭

## 其二

枯藤老树衰，

寒鸭戏水来。

依依不归去，

咋咋唤鸭儿。

# Ducks in Dusk

## Chapter 2

Old trees and rattans are all withered in autumn dusk.

In cold wind, wild ducks are just swimming back.

Why do they suddenly stop in the lake?

"Ga,Ga,Ga" , the mother duck is quacking to her baby duck.

# 暮鸭

## 其三

两道水纹斜斜裁，

一路向前徐徐开。

盈盈穿桥石下过，

茸茸小鸭露头来。

# Ducks in Dusk

## Chapter 3

Two oblique lines are tailored out on surface of the pond.

On the water, it straightly goes forward.

Surrounding a rock, passing a bridge, its running is so rapid.

Floating out of water, finally it is a baby duck's head.

# 春之灵

## 其一 春莺

微雨迷离春草生，

小塘水涨绿柳新。

君行林下轻步履，

寂寂春径藏春莺。

# Spring Spirits

## Chapter 1 Spring Warblers

Drizzle is sprinkling onto the new grasses.

Willows just turn green as water in pond rises.

My friend, please be quiet when walking in path.

Along the way, there are some spring warblers.

261

# 春之灵

## 其二 雏雁

春风袅袅举家出，

衔花啄草嫩羽舒。

绒绒几点下塘去，

前呼后合波上凫。

# Spring Spirits

## Chapter 2  Baby Geese

In spring wind, our family goes out to have fun .

We bite grasses and flowers although we are young.

Downy babies can swim in pond as spring is coming on.

Under parents caring, we are freely floating up and down.

263

# 春之灵

## 其三 春雁

绿柳满塘芦芽出，

荆花落雨滴素珠。

凌波一排乘风起，

画成春雁出水图。

# Spring Spirits

## Chapter 3 Spring Geese

Around pond, willows turn green and reed shoots are tender.

In raining, pure pearls drip down from the thorn flower.

A row of geese are flying up along the river.

It's just a charming picture of spring geese going out of water.

# 春之灵

## 其四 白鸥

素影如霜映碧塘，

穿林掠水自翱翔。

凌波舒爪捕鱼去，

春风一缕任飞扬。

# Spring Spirits

## Chapter 4 White Gull

Pure shadow as if frost is clearly reflected in clean water.

Passing trees and skimming water, it is in free flutter.

Over ripples, it rapidly seizes the fish without hover.

In a wisp spring wind, it is just a super flyer.

# 蓝山

  蓝山是多伦多周边著名的滑雪胜地。位于多伦多北部大约 1 小时半车程的地方，毗邻乔治亚湾最南端。山上有古老岩洞，是印第安民族早年居住的地方，风景优美。另外，山间有北美最长的一座索桥，横跨东西，也是观海览景的一处好去处。

# Blue Mountain

Blue Mountain is a very famous place to ski in winter. It is just 1.5 hours drive north of Toronto, closely up to the south of Georgian Bay, where there are some ancient caves that the Indian lived in. Across the valley, there is the longest suspension bridge in North America, where you can enjoy the wonderful views and vast sea.

# 岩洞

石开一方孔，地陷九尺阴。

蜿蜒蜷曲进，崎岖匍匐行。

洞天只眼大，岩影孤灯明。

当年人居此，夜夜海潮声。

# Rock Hole

A huge rock opened a rectangular hole,

which sinks about nine feet and the air become cool.

The space is so narrow that I have to wriggle.

The access is so winding that I move slow.

The small door is just as an opening eyebrow.

A lamp is faintly shining in the rock shadow.

Ancient Indian lived here many years ago.

They slept in each night as the tides come and go.

271

# 山行

逶迤穿萝径，谈笑望白云。

近海天远大，临崖山幽深。

古洞藏明暗，林壑转阴晴。

乘兴搜遐异，罗衫湿汗津。

# Going in Mountain

Walking on meandering, we pass the luxuriant creeping plants.
With harmonious talking, we savor the adrift white clouds.
Facing the vast sea, the blue sky appears more spacious.
Approaching steep precipice, the cliff is more dangerous.
In ancient caves, it is sometimes light and sometimes lightless.
In deep valley, it alternates brightness with darkness.
With high interests, we happily look for the wonderful views,
in spite of the sweat wets our clothes.

# 青涧

寒涧起氛阴，绿苔印石青。

晴天露一线，危崖百丈深。

巉岩千斤重，翠藤轻如风。

扪萝出幽壑，白云海上生。

# Deep Valley

In deep valley, there suffuse some cool mist.

With moss covering, the stones are so verdant.

Looking overhead, there is a thread of sky left.

Standing steeply, cliffs are hundred miles deep about.

Weighting almost thousand pounds, the huge stones are abrupt.

Swaying in breezes, the green vines are quietly light.

Climbing vines, we pass through the valley and then get out.

Over the sea, the white clouds slowly float.

# 蓝山石

此山养性灵，山中育石精。

琢磨出圆润，光照生彩虹。

团团盈手爱，玲珑若有情。

倾囊相求得，遥寄桂香人。

# Stones in Blue Mountain

Blue Mountain quietly embryos its spirit,

so that the spiritual stones are grown out.

After being polished, they became so smooth and cute.

In sunlight, they are rainbow-colored and brilliant.

Lovely balls holding in hand, they are so smart.

Brightening my eyes, they really charm my heart.

I decide to get them in spite of the cost,

for I would send them to my laurel-smelled sweet.

# 索桥

纤索系东西，飘摇过天梯。

凌空青峰小，踏虚云霞低。

澹澹海波静，渺渺天风吹。

悠然穿桥过，泉声响山石。

# A Suspension Bridge

From west to east, a suspension bridge hangs in shiver.

When lopping on it, it seems stepping on a fairyand ladder.

Standing in high space, the mountain peaks seem smaller.

Staying in the empty, the luster and clouds became lower.

In the far, the vast sea looks cleaner.

Around me, the breeze is just slighter.

Passing through the bridge, I'm a leisure traveler.

On the stones, a singing spring wells up a pool of clean water.

# 苏姗玛丽

　　苏姗玛丽是安大略省北部著名的旅游城市，市内著名的双彩虹桥连接美加两国。距离市区 110 公里的亚加华大峡谷是北美秋季赏枫最著名的地方。峡谷中风景秀丽，溪流潺潺，每年秋季，火红的枫叶把这里渲染成了一条鲜艳的峡谷。

# Sault Ste.Marie

Sault Ste. Marie is located in the north of Ontario; it's a famous city for travelling, where there is famous double-rainbow bridge closely connecting Canada and US. About 110 kilometers away the city, Agawa Canyon is the most famous place to view the maples in every autumn, it's characterized by clean river, verdant pines and colourful maples.

# 行车

临窗赏秋景，高峡穿长龙。

逶迤千山过，蜿蜒一壑中。

天淡红枫艳，峡阔暮云平。

彩虹落水处，长列徐徐停。

# Travelling on Train

By window, I enjoy the graceful view in autumn.

As if a huge dragon, the train runs downstream.

Passing hills and hills, the wagons slowly move.

In the deep canyon, they continuously creep.

Out of window, the maples are just aflame.

Above the train, the cloudy sky is so dim.

A charming rainbow falls into the stream,

where the train with its roar slowly stop.

# 攀崖

乘兴登崖顶，欲览五彩枫。

天阶行千众，仙台傍三松。

俯瞰一脉水，仰观两山云。

苍崖起骤雨，红叶落纷纷。

# Climbing Mountain

I climb up to the mountain top with high interests,

because I eagerly want to see the colourful maples.

So many guests are climbing on the heavenly steps.

The fairyland deck is closely up to three big pines.

Surveying the canyon, stream becomes narrow as my pulse.

Looking the sky, both mountains of canyon are all in clouds.

On the mountains top, the rain suddenly comes.

It causes the red leaves falling all over the mountains.

# 秋峡

秋峡骤雨停，霁色映红枫。

山在虹边隐，水从云中生。

溪声带疏雨，浅渚立长松。

青崖相对峙，簌簌起凉风。

# Canyon in Autumn

In autumn canyon, the sudden rain stops.

Faint sunshine spreads on the red maples.

Mountain peak hides in rainbow brilliance.

Clean stream originates from rows of clouds.

Stream still sings with scattering rain drops.

On small islet, a tall pine obliquely stands.

Mountains of both banks stand there face to face.

Only cool winds continuously blow the trees

# 素纱瀑布

苍崖吐素瀑，一派好画图。

洒空飞晴雨，冲虚亮银弧。

落水生秋雾，噙云润石枯。

殷殷枫红处，澹然景色殊。

# Bridal Veil Fall

The black cliff disgorges a pure fall.

Just as a painted scroll, it is so wonderful.

Spraying in space, sunny rain falls from the tall.

Rushing to the empty, it looks like a silvery bow.

Thin fog is diffusing up after it pours into a pool.

It mists the clouds and wets stones along the shore.

Numerous maples redden everywhere in the later fall,

but such elegant view is different from them at all.

# 黑狸瀑布

谁家素丝绸，挂在青山头。

随风散五股，临崖响三秋。

飒飒红叶落，淙淙水乱流。

观瀑松间坐，洗心涤烦忧。

# Black Beaver Fall

Whose pure silk is hanging over there?

It was left on the brae with no care.

As winds blow, it shares five plies in the air.

In later autumn, it still sings near Agawa gare.

Red maple leaves have fallen down everywhere.

Gurgling water is flowing as if scattering tear.

I enjoy the fall as pines diffuse fresh smell.

My heart is so calmed without any fear.

# 夜观苏珊玛丽大桥

玲珑星河灯，错落两岸明。

莹莹照秋水，翩翩映彩虹。

国近双虹引，水远五湖通。

良辰栖白鹭，素影落碧空。

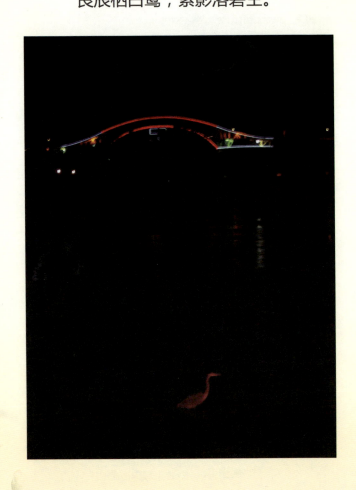

# Enjoying Sault Ste. Marie International Bridge in Night

Along the river, so many lamps are brilliant.

They scatter there and both banks are so bright.

Glitteringly, lights are shining along the autumn water.

Gracefully, lamps are seting off the charming rainbow arc.

Rainbow bridge connecting, the two countries are adjacent.

Flowing far, river links five lakes as a hydrographic net.

While a white heron is staying in water for having a rest.

It quietly stands there in so charming night.

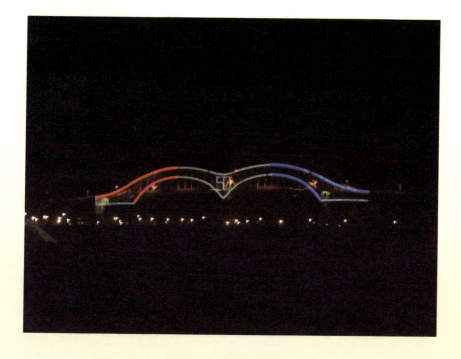

# 摩罗崖省级公园

摩罗崖省级公园是安大略省东南部的一个公园，距离多伦多大约 1 小时的车程。公园内树木茂密，溪流潺潺，悬崖耸立，是一处可以骑马，爬山，林中漫步的好去处。

# Mono Cliff Provincial Park

Mono cliff provincial park is located at south-east part in Ontario. It is about 1 hour drive of Toronto. In the park, there are stream, forest and steep cliff. It is a proper place for travelers to ride horse, climb cliff and walk in the trail.

# 与张志华秋游摩罗崖

微雨过秋河，青崖红叶飘。

疏林穿深径，野水平板桥。

日晚林塘静，山阴起云涛。

踟蹰将归去，彩虹一天高。

# Autumn Trip in Mono Cliff with Mr. Zhang, Zhihua

In drizzling, we cross the stream in spite of the tiny drips.

From the cliff, red leaves fell down all over the mountains.

Through the withered trees, there is a deep winding path.

Almost overflowing the small bridge, the stream quietly flows.

Dusk approaching, the pond in forest is just in calmness.

All the mountains become gloomier under the tumbling clouds.

We hesitate whether we should leave this bleak place.

Suddenly, a rainbow appears, as if all the world being in its brilliance.

297

# 诗意总在平常处

## 秋日赏花访友

闻说君家秋兰好，邀来朋党共一眺。

花浓似火灼灼俏，人淡如菊浅浅笑。

花开花谢春长在，秋去秋来天易老。

一生辛劳半生过，饮君清茶与君道。

# Poetic Living Just around Us

## Enjoying Flowers with Friends in Autumn

Hearing that your autumn cactus bloomed in peak.

I gathered old friends to go have a look.

The lushly blossomed flowers were aflame with red and pink.

You daisy-like hostess rippled sweet smiling on your cheek.

Flowers bloom and wither leaving no single spring's track

Autumn comes and goes hardly keeping the old days back.

Half a lifetime passed with all of our experienced hardship and luck.

Together we brewed a pot of green tea and freely had a talk.

# 冬日访友

最爱君家青枫林，飒飒雪风隔窗听。

春来长成千丛翠，夏至撑出十亩阴。

鸟啼鸟宿林常静，人去人来家最亲。

慢品香茗临窗坐，一壶春茶论古今。

# Visiting a Friend in Winter

Mostly I like the maples around your house row and row.

Beyond the window, could you hear winds are blowing snow?

When spring coming, thousands of green branches lushly grow.

In summer, they will offer you ten hectares of cool shadow.

Whether birds rest or sing, trees keep quiet as days flow.

No matter you host come or go, family mostly warms your soul.

Sitting by the window, we drink your spring tea and talk slow.

In our talking, stories in the past and present are passing through.

# 晚窗

小堂寂寂煎药饵，

秋阴未散云渐开。

久等闲客客不至，

彩虹映上晚窗来。

# Evening Views in Windows

In quiet drawing room, I am boiling the herbs.

Mists float in sky, there are rolling clouds.

Guest doesn't come though a long time passes.

While a brilliant rainbow lightens my windows.

**图书在版编目(CIP)数据**

诗一样的安大略/刘昭著.—上海:
上海三联书店,2013.4
ISBN 978-7-5426-4103-8

Ⅰ.①诗… Ⅱ.①刘… Ⅲ.①诗集-中国-当代-汉、
英 Ⅳ.①I227

中国版本图书馆CIP数据核字(2013)第016563号

# 诗一样的安大略

著　者/刘　昭

责任编辑/陈启甸　李　珏
装帧设计/今　申
监　　制/任中伟
责任校对/张思珍

出版发行/上海三联书店
　　　　(201199)中国上海市闵行区都市路4855号2座10楼
　　　　http://www.sjpc1932.com
印　　刷/上海图宇印刷有限公司

版　次/2013年4月第1版
印　次/2013年4月第1次印刷
开　本/890×1240　1/32
字　数/370千字
印　张/10
书　号/ISBN 978-7-5426-4103-8/I·678
定　价/108.00元